About the Author

Allan Jamieson has lived on four continents and he travelled widely prior to 1981, at which time he came to live on *the island*.

After retiring from employment in 1999, he wrote eight non-fiction books to document aspects of his experiences of the world:

2005 Emerging from the Past: A Family History with a Difference
2007 No Return: The Life of Rachel Newton (1803-1855)
2011 The Pulp: The Rise and Fall of an Industry
2013 Enthusiastic Amateurs: A Cautionary Tale for Golf and Sporting Clubs
2015 Honto Henro: The 88 Temple Buddhist Pilgrimage in Japan
2016 Meandering Mind: Short Stories
2017 Service above Self: The 75-year History of Burnie Rotary Club
2018 Voyage through the "Big Empty"

Now, after living half his life on *the island*, Allan has turned to fiction. In "*Surviving* is dead easy" he exposes the many advantages of the island's unique, valuable culture.

Surviving is

dead easy

by

Allan Jamieson

<u>*the Island*</u>

(area 64,500 km²)

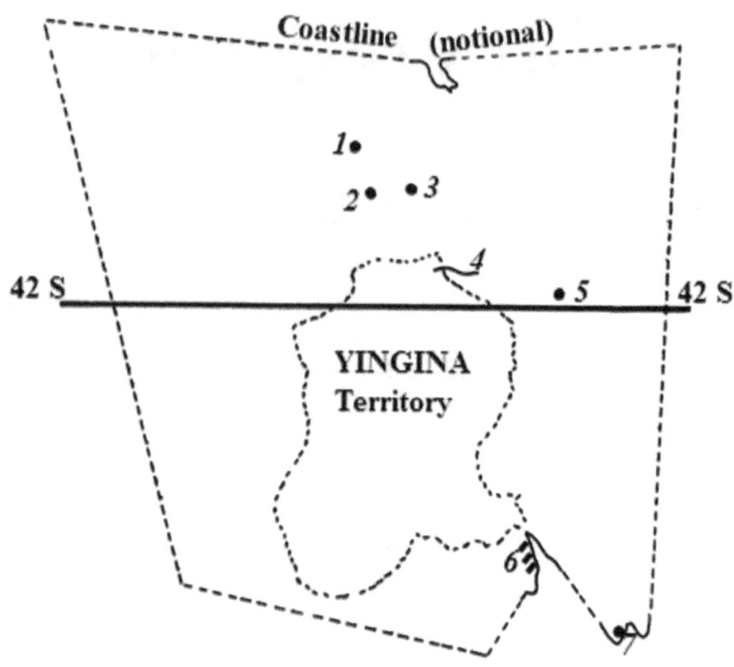

1 Paradise
2 Mole Creek
3 Deloraine
4 Brumby's Creek
5 Campbell Town
6 Old capital
7 Port Arthur

Map of the Old Capital

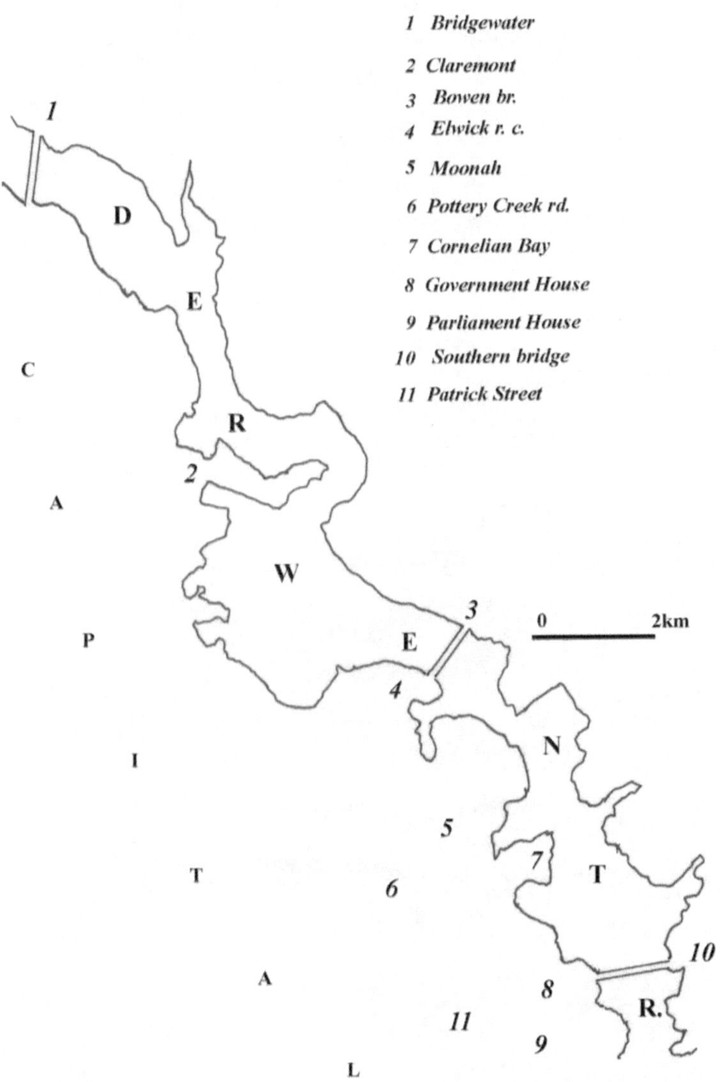

Preface

G'day, I'm Ned Youd and I've been pressured to set down a record of what my mate Tom Badcock and I experienced earlier this year. Tom and I are farmers; neither of us has done much reading or writing and the word "pressured" is certainly right in my case.

Tom and I were mates in school. Our farms are near, but not adjoining each other. We've grown closer in the past decade or so, after we found a common interest, searching for Restless ones in our spare time. For more on why we do this, I'll tell you later on.

This year is one century after the disastrous Restless culture was destroyed all over the world and billions of people died. For all we know, there might not be anyone alive anywhere except on this, our island. You could think there would not be any followers of the Restless culture still living here, but Tom and I do sometimes latch onto one.

For our pains, this year we found ourselves twice on the verge of being murdered – hence my story – but I'm getting ahead of myself.

Ned Youd, outside Mole Creek

October 2150

1-   <u>Paradise Fair</u>

May 21, 2150

Crack!

'Shit!'

Silence returned to the night.

In the dawn light, Tom and I walk the short distance to the path. We'd left our farms late yesterday afternoon and so spent the night just off the track through the forest to the north of where we live. The stick I'd placed there last evening is now in two pieces and Tom's rock is almost upside down.

'He had to be walking fast to have done that, Ned. No wonder he swore.'

'I reckon he was a Restless one. Nobody in our town would walk through the forest at night. Why the hurry?'

Quick as a flash, Tom says, 'Perhaps he had to leave Mole Creek all of a sudden. Want to lay a bet: a crook or Restless?'

We clear the path and head in the direction the stranger went. Our conversation is pretty much always one-sided; I'm tall, with a weight to match and I've always allowed my bulk to do my talking, but Tom is short – my eyes are drawn to his bald patch bobbing up and down in front as we walk in single file though the trees – and he expresses his thoughts rapidly all the time. He's a funny bugger. I've always known he was a talker, had been one since our school days, but I found we could work together on something; his words somehow stimulate my mind into action. Tom reckons I've still got my hair because I don't think much.

Tom's wife is quiet, thank goodness. I mean, there surely couldn't be two talkers in the one house. They have one son, who moved away many years ago and I don't hear Tom talk about him much these days. I'm separated from my wife and our two daughters found partners and moved to another Clan over 20 years ago. We are effectively free to do what we choose to, outside of running our farms. Searching for Restless ones happens to be our current interest in common.

'Just think, Ned; it is a hundred years since Western Civilisation vanished in a puff of smoke and you and I have seen sixty of those years go by.' I smile; it's his way of reminding me that his birthday was last week – I knew, but saw no point in commenting at the time.

'This path was once a road used by cars. The trees would have reclaimed it by now, except that it's a useful track and people keep it open.'

He said much the same last year. Cars were of no use here after the collapse, because worn out tyres could not be replaced; apart from a small amount of very low-quality coal, fossil fuels cannot be sourced on our island, so even electric cars were soon of no use.

We're walking on what was Union Bridge Road. Though a minor road, it enabled the communities living south of the forest to communicate with the farming areas north of the forest. Mother Nature has done an effective job of reclaiming this strip of land since the collapse. Tom and I clear away the few tree branches and small shrubs that threaten to complete the reclamation. I like to imagine that the small animals we heard last night appreciated our efforts as they scampered along.

Of course, time is not our enemy like it had been for the Restless ones, so it made more sense for us islanders to walk or use horses; we farmers soon realised that the simplest way to plough paddocks was to use horses or bullocks.

Ready for what I knew would come next; I manage to get a word in first. 'We never rid ourselves of horses, which was just as well. Chaff and leather is all we need to use *them* and there's plenty of rusting iron around, so we can make zillions of horse shoes!'

Tom doesn't miss a beat. 'Yes, we're well off here now.

Cotton had been brought to our island, but we replaced that with linen,' he said, 'because we had grown flax before the collapse. Sugar beet crops replaced imported sugar. Before the collapse, we had to import a lot of seafood, because companies exported so much of our fish and shellfish overseas that our own fishing grounds became depleted. However, after the collapse the fish stocks recovered and we don't have to limit the catch anymore.'

I nod. Though he cannot see my action, I know it is simplest to let Tom talk.

'What say, Ned? It's a while since a Restless one was caught. I'll bet this bloke's a crook; a thief or maybe the father of some girl is now hopping mad at him.'

'Silly bugger if that's the case.'

We're on our way to Paradise; not to the once-a-month gathering of farmers and other hopefuls, standing with produce laid out on rude tables, but to the once-a-year event held every May when just about everyone who comes to that town will have something to exchange. Bargaining is the main game. Tom is pleased with three matching pairs of clogs in the bag on his back. He told me he had spent a month whittling these and he's aiming to sell or trade them to some Dad, Mum and Child. Trading, though, is not our real purpose; we're searching for followers of the Restless culture and I sense that success might be ours again in 2150. The timing suits us, our crops are in and right now there's a short respite before we start farming again.

After walking a while down a slope in the forest, we come out of the trees and stand upon open land. As we walk between farms, Tom's remarks take my mind back to the tales we heard when we were young.

During the first half of the 1800's, 70,000 convicts were exiled here by Britain. The convicts could never hope to return home and the island was their one source of hope, providing a more positive future than Britain could ever offer. The convicts soon had fresh meat in abundance and their health was far superior to that of the poor people in England and Ireland who continued to live the only life the convicts had known.

By contrast, the intention of the much smaller number of wealthy free-settlers on the island at that time was to make money and return home to England.

I had asked Tom some years ago if he could recall what his Elder said concerning the influence of Irish convicts on our island's history and culture and I remember his response pretty well. It went more or less along these lines. Nowhere else in the world did convicts, former convicts and their descendants constitute the *majority* of a population over such a long time. At one time, around twenty per cent of prisoners arriving here came from Ireland. Tom told me the reason they were a significant group went back one thousand years ago, to when English nobles went to Ireland and forcefully took over large areas of land there. The Irish could only become tenants of these English. Irish tenants were worse off than slaves; each tenant *had* to pay his rent and landlords could dispossess their tenants even if they *did* pay their rents. Former tenants could not be given shelter by any other family on the estate. Trading and agriculture activities were not allowed the Irish; growing potatoes for own use was all they could do. Then, six hundred years after that land grab by the English, a severe frost destroyed the entire potato crop; a frightful famine ensued and some 400,000 people starved to death.

It is obvious that the Irish convicts who landed here had no love of the authorities – of the British – and as soon as the opportunity arose, they took their own culture and went "underground" in our forested areas. Their work practices were those from way before the Industrial Revolution.

For 250 years, the Restless ones in charge on our island had tried to dictate conditions, but Irish convicts showed all islanders how to cope with oppression by Restless ones. Today, around one-quarter of all islanders is of Irish descent.

Tom seems to know what I'm thinking – mental telepathy perhaps?

'The Industrial Revolution never truly reached us, Ned, so being on this remote island meant self-reliance would be the only feasible way of life. It is uncanny, or maybe it was Irish luck, but their lack of sophistication was exactly what was most beneficial when the Restless culture collapsed. Going back to basics was not hard for them. They'd resisted taking up all the whiz-bang ideas and machines pressed upon them by the Restless.'

'Yes', I said, 'It shows how apt the expression is; "The Future is in The Past."'

I am not sure Tom notices what I've said, for he continues; 'The rest of the world never knew how idyllic our climate is year-round; there hasn't been a glacier here for over 10,000 years! In one regard, the Restless culture did us a good turn – we have "oodles" of electric power, a genuine sustainable energy. Some parts of our island get up to five metres of rain a year, ideal for generating hydroelectric power, but the few factories we did have were forced to shut down when the collapse occurred – no customers, no ships – eliminating what had been a large demand for electricity and we've plenty now.'

We walk on and some buildings at Paradise come into view at a distance. When we reach the long main street, my ears start to be assaulted from all sides with the cut and thrust of haggling as I wander around.

'Four persimmons – what am I bid?'

...

'Come here Ladies; five skeins of wool, turn them into a winter pullover for your school age child. Which of you has an offer?'

...

'A dozen corn cobs for my son's trike? Throw your hat in and it's a deal.'

...

'Is this enough? There's six horseshoes in the bag.'
'Is the bag included?'

...

'I said to 'im, Edna, "that's mad, that is! I wouldn't give you 'alf for that old saddle", I said.'
'What'd 'e say?'
'He laughed and said I'd know what to do with me offer.'
'Ooh, rude bugger! Point 'im out to me.'

...

I can hear Tom's voice. 'Become this year's clogged-up family and stand out in the crowd.'

I spot a stranger holding a clock in one hand; he's on his own, not attracting a crowd. I surmise he's maybe 25 years old, taller than average. I walk over to him.

'G'day. Is that a clock?'
'Yes. You wind this one up and it never stops working.'
'I already know the time.'
'So, what time is it?'
Glancing up, I say, 'a bit after ten o'clock.'
'It's ten-forty. You're not bad, but you can't do that at night.'

I look around. No one's nearby. The bloke's a Restless one, I think, and not very bright. He might not be a danger, though he could be of value if he were to lead us to some mates – that's if he has any. I reply:

'If I can see the stars, I can judge the time to within 30 minutes – not that I ever worry about the minutes. Your clock is useless, so you won't get much for it.'
'When it's cloudy how do you get on?'
'It's enough to know that it's night time. By the way, why were you out walking at four o'clock this morning?'
'Why? Were you following me?'
'No, but my mate reckons you made some girl pregnant and were on the run from her father.'

He stammered, 'Yes – yes, as it happens, your mate was spot on.'

'I'll tell him. He and I made a bet. I reckoned you were a Restless one.'

'Oh, come on – they died out years ago.'

I drift away and take a circuitous route to where Tom is standing. 'I'm sure the bloke is on a journey, Tom.' Tom glances towards the fellow.

'Maybe he started in Yingina territory, Ned, and could well intend to return there, because it's in the centre of our island, with some thinly populated and mountainous parts. If there is a gang of Restless ones, I'd plump for them hiding in Yingina. Looks like he's hoping to contact someone, Ned; the clock is so that person will know who he is.'

'That means he doesn't know this other person.'

Tom drifts over to talk to the stranger and I get within earshot behind the bloke.

'What do you want for your clock?'

'It's a beauty. I want a good deal for it.'

'OK. How about I exchange this pair of clogs for your clock? They're the right size for you, I'd say, and you'll get some use out of them, which is more than I will get from your clock.'

'Then, why do you want the clock?'

'I could be a better salesman. I could trade it for something better before I leave here today, but I also have a friend who collects clocks on the quiet. He has his reasons.'

'I'll accept your exchange if you promise to give my clock to your friend.'

'Scout's honour!'

I begin to follow the stranger. Perhaps his task is to make contact with other Restless ones, *outliers* so to speak, and urge them to join the main band. Will we catch two Restless ones, or was Tom's transaction observed? Paradise Fair has been a good venue for us in the past; all sorts of people congregate here and random conversations take place all the time.

When I return, Tom still holds the clock.

'Our friend has headed south, Tom, back the way he came and he's not wasting time. It supports your theory!'

'The clock rattles if I shake it. I want to open it up.'

We head homewards, stopping at the slow-moving Minnow River to do a bit of fishing before spending the night there. Tom gets a screwdriver out of his bag.

'Come here, Ned.'

Tom hands me a small locket. There's no chain attached, but when I open it, a piece of paper, folded tight, falls out.

'We've had a win after all, Tom. The paper asks the recipient to return both locket and clock to an address in Yingina.'

2-   <u>My Elder's Notes</u>

The Elders are very important in maintaining our island's culture. For instance, they provide teenagers – those about to finish their schooling – with details of the Restless culture and why we islanders need to guard against that culture re-emerging here. Almost fifty years ago, an Elder gave me lessons. I was in my last school year and she was very thoughtful, because she gave us students a set of notes each and said, "Take care of these; they'll help you recall *why* the Restless culture must not again dominate our island."

I know that our Island culture originated well before the culture of the Restless; our rhythm is controlled by the sun and the moon. It's a simple life that we can manage.

About ten years ago, I stumbled upon these notes in my home, re-read them and showed them to Tom. His Elder hadn't been so well prepared, though it was clear that Tom had retained details of his Elder's lessons better than I had of my lessons. We decided to spend a few days after the harvest each year looking for Restless ones.

Here are my Elder's notes:

Why the Restless Destroyed their Civilisation

The Restless were called that because they were never still, always trying to achieve more in a day. They drove their cars everywhere, always in a hurry; their day was divided into hours, minutes, seconds, milliseconds. To them it was important to go further, faster, higher every day. Nature was in their way. They *thought* they were in control. Now, they are no more.

<u>A Milkmaid's Stool has three legs</u>

Three legs provide stability. The Restless culture was supported by a kind of three-legged stool, the legs being Technology, Politics and Economics. The failure of any one leg would bring about the collapse, however the actual collapse came not as a result of a single event; a one-word explanation is inadequate.

<u>Leg 1</u>: Technology

Knowledge has no overt value; only when someone makes use of knowledge can value be created. The application of knowledge is called technology. The patent system reveals how fast technology expanded. You could be awarded a patent if you proved that you were the first to make use of some knowledge. The holder of a patent had an exclusive right to exploit this idea for a long time. A patent had value! The first patent was issued in America in 1790 and during the next 100 years, an average of five patents were being issued per day, but in 2020, around 8,000 new patents were being issued somewhere in the world every day!

There was no *will* to stop and advances in technology of machines, medical procedures, genetic engineering, marine science, digital electronics, aerospace, etc. took the Restless culture right to the brink of destruction.

Typical of technology was the fact that much planning went into sourcing and selection of any raw materials, but much less attention was paid to effluents and wastes from the process. In short, the *consequences* of the technology.

Here's an example of what one innovation could lead to. The invention of the steam engine was of great benefit to mankind, but later, mankind experienced what it must have been like on a runaway train – the people were helpless in the wake of all the countless changes that followed thick and fast:

- 1830: A steam engine is first used in England to haul a train
- Later, other steam engines drive machines in factories
- Factories are located in cities and country people flock to cities to work
- Cities quickly become totally dependent on poor, peasant

farmers to grow the food they need.

\- City people <u>become</u> Society; Farmers become *non* people.

Technology's role in the collapse in 2050 followed an "electronic intelligence" path:

> \- In the second half of the 20th Century, electronics experts succeeded in enabling computers to communicate with each other
> \- Computer networks began to automate machines that were remote from each other
> \- Over half of all people lived in cities, dependent on a diminishing number of elderly farmers to grow and supply them with food
> \- Automation stepped in; large, multi-national companies purchased or leased farms, running them remotely thanks to their capacity to employ automation, not people
> \- Total reliance was soon placed on internet computer networks to check soil moisture, weed infestations, etc., while harvesting machines travelled through paddocks followed by trucks able to wash, pack and transport the produce to city supermarkets – all by remote control, untouched by human hands – the ultimate triumph of technology
> \- Cities became fully dependent on this widely automated system working as intended – it could not *be* switched off
> \- Farms no longer *saw* people!

Those who developed the computer networks never had a monopoly on cleverness; it was just that they *thought* they did and the general public did not know enough to call their bluff. All internet systems were created by human beings hence it would only be a matter of time before *other* human beings – nicknamed 'hackers' – could figure out how to corrupt these systems so they would not work.

<u>Leg 2</u>: Politics

In the sixth century BC, the Greeks had a word, 'democracy' to describe their concept of government. *Some* people (specifically city-dwelling adult males) could vote on laws by a show of hands at public gatherings.

In the early days of what became the Restless culture at the end of the 17th Century, the democracy concept was seriously corrupted when political *parties* were invented. From then on, the public gave up their control to a party's leaders – a clique – who occupied the top layer of the party, well separated from the unwashed mass of voters. The clique's focus was on preserving power; promises made at the last election were forgotten!

An interesting sequence of events took place over the next three centuries:

- The cliques were content for the public – the voters – to be uneducated, but factory owners needed workers who could read, write and – more and more – think
- The traditional providers of education had been religion-based and unwilling to change, but governments began to build and run schools to satisfy the owners
- From late in the 19th century, government schools began to dominate education, which became compulsory and over time the populace gradually became an educated one
- By 2010, the majority of educated people in developed countries realised that they held one important power – the *right* to vote
- Parliaments typically comprised two political houses; the lower house was where laws were proposed and where the laws would be proclaimed, provided the members in the upper house voted in favour of the laws
- In several elections around the world in 2016, voters did not focus on getting a political *party* into power in the lower house; instead the voters reasoned they would gain more by forcing whichever party was in power to negotiate with *independent* politicians who tended to congregate in the upper house and who were always ready to listen to the public.

[Voters on our island had always been in a favourable position in this regard. Our Upper House comprised a *majority* of Independent members and, for well over one hundred years prior to the collapse, the party in power in the Lower House on our island *always* had to design its legislation so that sufficient *independent* Upper House Members – by nature cautious of "development" – would agree with it.

After the collapse, these Members abolished the Lower House and political parties ceased to exist. Consensus, not naked power, rules our island.

Clan Elders ensured we would continue to have a good, broad education base, because this would restrict the ability of any one person or group of persons to lead our people in a direction they did not want to take.]

Leg 3: Economics

In the 20th Century, two diametrically opposed economic theories, "Bretton Woods" and "Neoliberalism" held sway in different periods:

Bretton Woods (1944-1971) arose when 44 nations, including America, agreed to fix the value of their currencies to that of gold and to restrict efforts to profit from monetary speculation
- As a consequence, debt levels in these countries dropped dramatically and investment was made in productive enterprises, leading to full employment
- In 1971, America deliberately withdrew from the Bretton Woods agreement
Neoliberalism (1971-2150) took over, allowing speculation to run riot and banks lent money to anyone who asked
- Politicians everywhere created new laws giving banks and financial institutions freedom to set rules contrary to the well-being of the general public; Australia's $44 billion life insurance industry made sure that it didn't have a code of conduct, it was granted exemptions from laws banning unfair terms in contracts, and it had the power to discriminate between customers

- In 2008, a large US investment bank collapsed due to its wildly irrational investment scheme, causing share markets in many countries to collapse as well
- Politicians panicked; printing massive amounts of money with value based on thin air, not on gold and effectively penalising people reliant on government welfare assistance and especially people yet to be born, by saddling the latter with an impossibly large debt burden.

This table shows one consequence of the application of the two theories in America.

<u>Average *annual* increase in income</u>
(after adjusting for inflation)

Theory	Bretton Woods	Neoliberalism
Period	1944 – 1971	1971 – 2008
"haves"*	$3,000/ann	$15,100/ann
"have nots"**	$670/ann	$77/ann

*top 1 per cent of population
**bottom 99 per cent of population

The small group of people at the top of the three-legged stool thought Neoliberalism was a good idea – there were no rules to enforce what should have been common sense and plain decency. Their selfishness was all that mattered to them. Neoliberalism righted the balance for the "haves" by ruining the lives of everyone else!

- By the time of the 2008 financial crisis, the US finance sector was providing 45 per cent of all US business profit, compared to less than 20 per cent of profits before the mid-1980s, clear evidence of a massive shift away from the traditional basis of the Industrial Age; employing people to produce goods
- In the early 21st Century, the 62 richest people in the world together held as much wealth – wealth that arose from the Rest-

less culture – as the 3,600 million people at the bottom half of mankind
- These "haves" were not punished.

<u>The Collapse in 2050</u>

People immersed in the Restless culture never saw that the end was coming:

> - Nine hundred years prior to the collapse, several religious wars (*later* termed Crusades) occurred when Christian armies invaded Islamic lands intent on, and succeeding in, inflicting maximum cruelty and murder on this 'enemy'
> - Feeling victimised for 900 years does not make for a contented life
> - One day in 2001, a terrorist group claiming allegiance to Islam succeeded in hijacking four aeroplanes in America and crashed three of these into iconic buildings of Western Civilisation; the hijacker's unspoken message being "You're Fools to Think You Can Stop Us!"
> - Other people, dissatisfied with the dictatorial attitude of Western Civilisation, looked for a way to exploit a technological "blind spot" – the fact that city people could only survive if the technology of automated growing and delivery of food continued to be applied
> - In 2016, some "hackers" demonstrated an ability to corrupt internet computer networks and soon these people were being controlled by opponents of Western Civilisation
> - America was the first nation to build an atom bomb, a devastating nuclear weapon, and for 100 years, it was the only country to use this weapon against other people
> - A great many other countries saw value in having their own atomic bombs.

The world had become unstable. Politicians should have played the key role in ridding the world of this threat, but the Restless culture ensured that international politics would encourage an *aggressive* stance, because only the most selfish and egotistical persons could rise to power within that culture.

The populations in developed countries were ageing and it became obvious that an ever-increasing number of citizens would have to depend on the government for their wellbeing, boosting demand for spending on health, public pensions and long-term care, but where was this money to come from? Ten years before the collapse, close on two-thirds of all countries had negative credit ratings; only madmen would loan them money. Vast amounts of pension fund monies were invested in government bonds, yet now nobody in their right mind would rely on their government. The pension system did not survive; the middle class, dominant in number terms, was the most affected. These people had worked throughout their adult life in the expectation, either that their own savings would fund their retirement, or that the "government" would supply pensions adequate to fund a comfortable life.

Thus, it was predestined that the Third World War would start, triggered by these three vulnerabilities coinciding in time:

1. Civil wars broke out within some countries – initiated when the majority of their citizens realised there was no way they could live, because their own savings had become worthless and their nations were financially bankrupt. The citizens blamed the politicians. The effect was to weaken these countries to their foundations.

2. The financiers, bankers and economists, who had created a world based on "Monopoly money" instead of being based on real assets, ran for cover; they had no means of correcting the financial collapse.

3. The controllers of the hackers let these loose to disrupt the remotely controlled farming systems and stop the transport networks of the developed world.

This third event was the last straw. America was quick to strike back at the countries they suspected; rockets armed with nuclear bombs headed to cities in China, the Arab nations, etc.. Within hours, atomic bombs were heading back from a dozen countries to fall on American and European cities.

Atomic weapons don't kill with their powerful blast wave alone; radiation carried around the world by the wind is itself lethal and people died for decades afterwards, despite living hundreds of kilometres from where the bombs landed.

All the aggression was confined to the northern hemisphere. Our island is located in the southern "roaring 40's" and the wind blows from west to east here more or less all year round. For a century prior to the collapse of the Restless culture, an atmospheric air quality monitoring station on our west coast demonstrated that our air quality was the purest in the world. The overwhelming majority of air pollution had been produced in the northern hemisphere, but almost none of this made it to our southerly latitude. So it was with atomic radiation as well.

===//===

The Restless culture has left a legacy; we are no longer ignorant and we can control our own life through the knowledge built up during that culture. It is <u>essential</u> that we – everyone – think through the consequences of acting on that knowledge – indeed on *any* knowledge – *before* we act.

From your Elder
June 2110

I was grateful for her dedication. She also told me how, after the collapse, the distribution of people on our island was quite different to what it had been. This meant that new political boundaries were needed. Fifteen new electoral districts – called 'Clan territories' now – were each assigned a name derived from our island's aboriginal heritage, rather than perpetuate the former names that reflected English surnames or place names. Each territory has a group of Elders who report to their relevant Upper House Member.

Cont'd →

3-   <u>A Yingina Chinwag</u>

'Tom, I know you change where you put some vegetables from one year to the next, but do you always plant the same ones somewhere on your farm?'

'The staple vegetables sell well, but I don't have to exercise my brain to grow them; like walking – one foot goes in front of the other without me *telling* it to do that. That's why I also allocate space each season to try one new plant, new for me, that is. There's two risks; the new plant might not grow well and the people might not want it even if does do well. However, I do this chiefly to give myself a mental challenge.'

This is where Tom and I differ. Somehow, I find myself absorbed by routine, day-by-day tasks and my brain isn't able to disentangle itself and be free to think of other things.

We'd left our farms early this morning and we are on our way to get to Brumby's Creek. It's easy going now, but we'll have to tackle the escarpment of the Western Tiers later to get to where the creek starts.

The sun moves past north. We've commenced our climb. Gradually the going is getting more difficult and we pause a while.

'Ned, look back now. We must be 600 metres above the Midland Plain!'

'Yes, but this path is just a goat track. It can't hurt to go through the trees instead.'

'Two hours ago the going was easy, but I'm thinking that this commune of the Restless, or whatever it's called, has to be around here somewhere. They'd not want to make it easy for islanders to find them.'

We're now on the escarpment. After some time among the trees, we arrive at what we reckon is Brumby's Creek and

Tom points upstream, 'there's the spot – that cliff face about 400 metres from here. There'd be water at the base and from the cliff you'd have a wide view along the Tiers. Let's split up and take a dekko. You go to the top and try not to be seen.'

'The trees up there are more like shrubs; your height! *You* go.'

Staying among the trees, I start walking up the slope, about 20 metres away from the creek. The only sound is babbling water.

'Where's your mate?'

The stranger from Paradise appears from behind a tree. He's wearing the same clothes he wore at Paradise, but so am I – I guess neither of us is out to impress anyone.

'He's behind you.'

The bloke laughs. 'You can't fool me that easily. Which one of you has the clock?'

'I'm not used to answering questions from strangers. I'm Ned. What's your name?'

'Here, I'm called Nigel. Now, where's the clock?'

'It's in safe keeping. If you're sensible, you'll get it back.'

'This is our territory. We will decide how to deal with you. Come and meet some Restless ones.'

Nigel strides uphill on the northern side of the creek. I follow until we are under an overhang in the cliff face. I realise I'm looking into a cave as my eyes adjust to the dim light. Some 15 or 20 men sit facing me. One of them stands up. He's in his sixties, I guess, medium height and well dressed, in contrast to everyone else I can see. He says, 'Our plan worked a treat. You collect clocks for your own reasons, I gather. What reasons?'

The hairs rise on the back of my neck. 'Am I right in thinking that you sent Nigel to Paradise to catch the two of us?'

He smiles, 'Got it in one!'

'Are we that important or dangerous?'

'Let's say you two are thorns in our socks. We want to eliminate this nuisance. However I am curious. What drives you to keep chasing us? If we do get rid of you, will some others pop up to take your place? If that were to happen, I don't see that we'll have gained anything.'

'What's your name?'

'Here, I'm called Robert.'

'Okay, Bob, I can assure'

'It is Robert!'

'Okay! Then, here I'm called Edward – got that Nige? Edward!'

'I'm Nigel, remember? Robert is waiting – we haven't got all day!'

'Is that a fact? I reckon you have a nice set-up here at peace with the world, no passing traffic, plenty of water, a view to die for, a roof over your heads, out of the wind and plenty of native animals and trout to catch and eat too. Don't tell me those clocks of yours drive every second of your day!'

I hear a noise behind me and Tom saying, 'What's this?' I turn and see he's surrounded by several men.

'Robert, allow me to introduce Thomas. Tom, this is Robert and that's Nige over there. It might not look it, Tom, but this is a formal place – like Buckingham Palace was said to be – except that we haven't had to curtsy to anyone. Does your accommodation have a name, Robert?'

'Camp twenty-one.'

'I might have guessed. I reckon you Restless ones are now a wandering tribe, just like the original inhabitants here. Right through the last Ice Age they survived, isolated and sur-rounded by glaciers. Nobody told them what to do and they managed without having any clocks. They had established what I'm told was the world's last remaining self-governing society, unknown to everyone. For thirty thousand years, this island was their home, but your ancestors, with their Restless culture of mindless aggression came here and annihilated this society in a mere three decades just over 300 years ago.'

'Ned, what's going on?'

'Good question. I'm trying to work that out. Seems Robert wants to know why you and I keep chasing Restless ones. He'd like us to stop, but he's worried we'll be followed by other Restless hunters. You tell him.'

'Most people think there are no Restless ones left – maybe a handful at most, but Ned and I keep finding them. Must admit though, we've never found twenty five at one time before! The plain fact is that if Ned and I were to somehow disappear, the people in our Clan would soon react. You can't be so wedded to your Restless culture that you've never noticed an important feature of our island's culture: information, true or false, travels by word of mouth fast from one end of the island to the other. We islanders *are* close-knit! There are others like us in other territories and rest assured Ned and I would soon be replaced by new Restless chasers in our own territory.'

'Tom's right; islanders survived without the telephone, the radio and that other invention of your culture, the internet. Until one hundred years ago, all those things were here and we could choose to use them, but we never *needed* them. Your culture proved toxic to the World. Acknowledge this and start living like us islanders do and Tom and I will stay on our farms.'

As guests, I realise that we are not being polite, yet Robert remains passive. Anyway, I'll place our opinions in front of him until he says "Stop". Of course, silencing Tom is another matter.

'Just in case you didn't quite understand what Ned implied, Bob, we accept strangers here, provided they don't seek to have us change the way we live. That's what saved us islanders from caving in to your culture three hundred years ago; your ancestors were always pushing and prodding us to support some newfangled scheme, to buy a new gadget or to take up some novel idea, yet we just toyed with those things.'

Yes, I thought, passive resistance was effective one hundred years ago too, after the collapse, when city people found themselves on what to them was foreign soil, the island's countryside. The city had become a useless address – starvation territory – and former city residents were ostracised in country towns unless they cast aside their old ways and "pitched in" rather than try to *change* their new neighbours.

Tom continued, 'Your Restless culture created a complex society everywhere dominated by city dwellers. From their vantage point it was easy for them to ride roughshod over the natural environment. In short, we islanders never saw your culture as civilised. A century later, we haven't changed our view.'

'That may be, but my fellows here can't undo what happened all those years ago.'

'Ned and I aren't asking that. Of course, you can't, Bob, but it is the Restless *culture* we are hunting. While you adhere to your horrible culture, we and others will hound you. Do as Ned says: Reject your culture and accept ours in its place.'

'I believe our behaviour proves we have made the switch.'

'Bullshit, Bob! A culture runs deep. You are keeping your fist hidden, but Ned and I can see you have one. Change means change everything, you can't pick and choose. Clocks are nothing but a laughing matter to us, but time was ever the Number One Commandment of your Restless culture: Thou shalt never waste a minute! Expecting us to use your formal names instead of what would be your normal names here, Nige and Bob, is a revealing sign that your fist is ever-present. It is a case of all or nothing.'

Time to go, I think. 'Robert, if it is all right by you Tom and I will be on our way now.'

All of a sudden, we are surrounded, our arms pinned behind us. Robert smiles. 'Separate them and tie their wrists behind their backs. The big one will come with me. Nigel, you're responsible for the little one.'

Robert and around ten others move in unison with me in their midst. We cross the creek using stones where we can and head into the forest. Soon, we come across a path.

'Where does this lead, Robert?'

No answer. I glance at the bloke on my left. He's rather thick-set, not as tall as I am; someone I'd describe as dependable.

'What's your name?'

'Here, I'm called Wayne.'

'So, when you're not here, everyone calls you John, I suppose.'

No answer. I am wasting my breath. The path is well used and follows the contours pretty well. We are gradually descending and the walking is easy. I estimate our overall direction is southwards, though there are twists and turns along the way.

After a fair while, we reach a small creek. Robert stops and explains, 'This runs into Weston's Rivulet, Edward. Do you know this area?'

'No, I don't, but I saw that name on a map when I was searching for Brumby's Creek.'

'Good, because you'll have plenty of time to get to know it. Tie him to the chain, Wayne. We'll be back this way in nine months' time – start of the autumn season next year, Edward. Don't go away!'

Guffaws reveal the group's amusement as they all move away heading further south.

Let's think things through, there's no point in panicking. Clearly, I'm in a real pickle. Some local farmer or blacksmith made the chain and it seems well-made. It isn't fixed to the tree nearest me, but wraps around it and both ends are tied somehow to my wrists. The tree trunk, though, is a good 40cm thick and I reckon the tree is about 20m high; it wasn't necessary to fasten the chain to the tree for it to be effective! I can't figure out how I am tied to the chain and I can't feel how my wrists are bound together either; this *has* to be the weak point of my bondage and I'll have to work out how to test it.

The path intrigues me. Maybe this mob of Restless ones don't come this way often, but somebody does, judging from its well-kept appearance. How long might I have to wait? It's nearing dusk. I'll make a comfortable bed for myself while I can see to do this and allow my brain – such as it is – to work on my predicament while I sleep. Fortunately, the chain is long enough to allow me to pile bracken and ferns together with my feet, sufficient for my comfort I trust, and I can reach the water in the creek. I'll just have to pee in my pants. Tomorrow is another day, *the* day when I have to get free.

***

Dawn! I'm stiff, my left leg's numb, my pants are wet, I've slept in fits and starts and I can't feel my hands. I've no bright ideas to try, so it looks like turning out to be a long day!

The one thing I can see to do is to inspect the chain, link by link, as maybe it isn't quite as well-built as it first appeared. Of course, success with this would mean I could get free from the tree, however dragging this long chain behind me would be bloody hard work and I don't know the shortest route to get help, except that it will be downhill from here.

I look at the sun – nine o'clock or thereabouts. Unfortunately, the chain is fit for purpose. I could use it on my farm, but I'd have to break it open first and I can't see any weak link.

I wonder how Tom's faring. My strength is my strength, though I can't bust the chain, but Tom's a resourceful little bugger. Mental telepathy would be useful right now. My sense is that Nige went in a different direction to Robert and that would be smart. We're a pretty effective team when we're together, Tom and me.

How can I get an arm free from whatever is binding my

wrists? With my back to the tree, I bang my wrists against the trunk – *clink, clink* – a metal sound, but maybe it's just chain links hitting together; I'm none the wiser about the binding.

Curse this chain! It's not long enough. I can see a fractured rock that could be useful as a makeshift knife, but it's just out of reach of my feet; the other stones nearby are all well-worn, with no edges.

Wait a moment! I walk to the creek. Yes, it's there – a bottle I glimpsed yesterday; an old Coke bottle by its shape. Maybe a Restless one tossed it away. That would be typical of them, always throwing things away with no thought of the consequences. Suddenly, I'm amused. What if the action a hundred or more years ago by one Restless bloke were to give me the chance to escape from this present gang of Restless ones!

I fish the bottle out with my left foot. It's unbroken, a pity, but after a while I figure out a way. With one foot, I place the bottle against the largest rock I can reach and then with my back to the bottle, I manage to raise the chain and drop it on the bottle. Raise and drop, raise and drop, raise and drop.

I realise this won't work; the bottle hasn't broken. Instead, I manage with my feet to lean the bottle against another rock and then jump on the bottle. Jump, jump. The bottle keeps slipping sideways and all I'm doing is working up a sweat.

Voices! Robert and Wayne appear, smiling.

'Did you find my little joke amusing?'

'You bastard, Bob. No, I did not and you can tell John Wayne to wipe the stupid grin off his face.'

'I thought as much. You two convinced me that you won't give up your campaign against us, so I thought I would show you what you are up against. We are well organised and we have plans for this island; plans that don't include you two.'

'What have you done with Tom?'

'Oh, you two can compare notes when you get home. Wayne, undo your handiwork, please.' Wayne goes behind me and is careful not to let me see how he had tied my hands togeth-er.

With a smile, Robert says, 'If it is all right by you, Wayne and I will be on our way now.'

'You'll keep!'

Cont'd 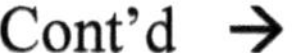

4-   <u>**Thinking Time for Ned and Tom**</u>

Almost home! That ordeal knocked the stuffing out of me and it has taken a real effort to keep walking. As I head past Tom's farm, I see him in the middle of his multi-crop paddock, the smallish area in which he rotates some of his better selling varieties of vegetables. Stepping, almost stumbling, over the fence, I call out, 'Tom, what happened to you?' Stopping, he stands upright and uses the handle of his hoe for support.

'I went to your place this morning, but you weren't there. I guess I got back home before you did.'

'Too right you bloody did! I haven't *been* home yet, but – again – what happened to you?'

'Nigel waited until Robert and you were out of sight, then I was hemmed in by twelve Restless ones. They led me down Brumby's Creek to a spot below where you and I had decided to split up. Incidentally, I succeeded in getting close to the top of the cliff without seeing anyone, but they had spotted me, because I was approached from behind! I think they must have sat waiting on the ground. Ten of them. How did you get on, Ned?'

I recount my experience, which Tom finds intriguing and humorous. The funny side is beyond me; my lack of sleep adds to my irritation and Tom still hasn't told me what he'd experienced.

'For the third bloody time, what happened to you?'

'I had it easier, Ned. As I was about to say, we left the creek and turned north to climb out of the slight gully. We were in the forest and it surprised me to see several paths. It was the evidence of recent use that struck me. Perhaps that part of Yingina territory is now home to Robert's band and they've several camps; we saw nobody else before they caught us. Maybe Robert – or whoever his boss is, if Robert's not the leader – arranged for all the tribe to stay at home in their camps while he set his trap for us.'

I'm a bit higher up the slope and standing erect so my bulk will be obvious, I shout, 'you're trying my patience, you know. What I need is sleep. You're avoiding telling me your story. What happened?'

He takes a step back, looking up at me.

'Nigel stopped in a part of the forest a little more open than most of the area. I was blindfolded, turned around some ten times to make me giddy and Nigel bid his farewell. I heard movement as the gang left me then it was silent.

'I had to rid myself of the blindfold and this I did by accident; slowly, I walked forward and collided with a tree. I hoped there'd be a branch stub or some protrusion on it that I could manage to slide under the blindfold and so prise it off. In a couple of minutes I'd succeeded.

'Of course, unlike you, I could walk anywhere I chose to and I'd seen that your wrists had been tied with a leather thong. I assumed mine were too, so I went in search of a sharp object. After a while, I saw a rock outcrop and part of it had split apart. There was a sharp edge, at almost the right height too, so I could work away while standing with my back to the rock.'

He holds his hands up, the hoe resting on his shoulder.

'I cut myself on the rock, of course – look – but when the thong was almost worn through I could bust it apart. That was a relief!'

'Bloody Hell! Nigel let you off lightly!'

'Yeah, Nigel and I are business acquaintances, remember? He was wearing the clogs I swapped for his clock. I thought of searching for you, but it was nigh on dark by then, so I found a good spot to lie in and I slept rather well. I didn't wet my pants – sorry, Ned. In the morning, I reasoned that you'd be free like me, so it was smarter to head home than to waste a lot of time trying to find you.'

'I could challenge that, but it is clear our next step is to talk to some of our territory's Elders.'

'Before we do, Ned, there are some questions I'd like to have answered; for instance, why did Robert set out to get us to Brumby's Creek?'

'I reckon he sees us as his main enemy, perhaps the one real enemy he and his mates have had to face so far and he wanted to meet us and size us up before he exposes his existence to the whole island.'

'Ah, "Better the Devil you know …" sort of thing. Do you think he's close to launching an attack on us islanders, then?'

'Soon, I reckon, because he ran a risk in showing his hand, Tom – I mean, he could not have expected us to back off and leave him alone once we'd seen the force he commands. He'd reckon we'll run to our Elders and if he sat on his hands, he'd be overrun by our forces.'

'So, a pre-emptive strike by him must be on the cards. What's our weak point?'

Premptive was a word I hadn't heard before, so I say what is most on my mind.

'Inertia would be part of it. It could take us islanders a month or so to get a strike force organised and start searching for him. We've only got Camp 21 identified. Who knows where else he has strongholds?'

'Campbell Town is his target, you'd think, Ned. That's where our Members congregate and it is wide open, defenceless. For a century, we've never imagined having to defend our Capital. If he was to pick a time when all Clan Members are in the Assembly Room, he could capture the whole lot. We know Restless ones can be hard to identify on their own and many of them could just walk into the town as individuals without generating suspicion.'

'That could well be the real reason he set the trap for us.

We'd be able to request an emergency meeting of all territory Members.'

'*Wow!* We need a different strategy, Ned. Can we persuade our Elders to convey information directly to their counterparts in all the other territories before the Members are asked to intervene?'

'Even better, each Member could be well informed without having to go to Campbell Town to be briefed and the Members could even conduct their decision-making work by means of 'petitions' on paper, which some Elders would carry to each territory for signing.'

While we've been talking, we've walked across the paddock towards Tom's house. The day is drawing to a close and there's no warmth in the sun any longer. He is still talking, but all I long for is sleep.

'I can see a job for us. Our farms may have to lie fallow for a couple of months or more while we spy out the enemy's territory.'

'We've little choice, Tom.'

'Yeah, but you have a cattle farm. Your animals may be dumb, but they can look after themselves quite well.'

'I've five hectare of crops to think about as well, you know that.'

Tom swings one arm in a wide circular motion. 'So? My whole 20ha is devoted to cropping. Nothing planted, nothing sold! All you ever do is stick your arm up some poor cow's backside, but be honest, Ned, she's the one doing the work!'

'You're nothing but a poor sharefarmer; growing vegetables is women's work – always has been. Shovelling cow shit around your carrots is your destiny, chum. Be like me and buy some cattle.'

'And, I bet you have just the herd to offer me too. Then, you could go hunting Restless ones all year round.'

'Don't be silly! Think what fun we've had. Money isn't

everything! Be honest, Tom, together we're a formidable team.'

I sense that Tom is also quite affected by yesterday's experience. I put my arm around his shoulders and squeeze. He reacts instantly; 'Oh, so now we're on our best Queen Victoria advice-to-women phase are we? "Lie back and think of England."'

'If I wasn't twice your size, I'd beat you up.'

'Brawn without brain is piss-weak, Ned. Remember, I didn't wet my pants.'

I stop and say, 'Okay, we're mates.'

'One other thing concerns me, Ned. What if there is an active Restless cell overseas and they're in contact with Robert's mob?'

'You think someone might have come ashore on our island unobserved?'

'That wouldn't be hard if the person was transported here on a yacht that didn't stay around, but went away again. Alternatively, maybe Robert is in radio contact with the cell. We islanders haven't switched on our radios for generations; there was nothing to listen to, but amateur radio used to be a hobby. You'd build your own transmitter and you could try to contact other amateur enthusiasts via their own radio sets. I'll bet some of those old radios still work. Robert might be aware that an invading force is about to arrive here.'

'*Shit!* Things would get serious and quickly, wouldn't they! We've no time to waste, Tom, but I'm too tired and irritable now to do more. Let's contact our Elders first thing in the morning.'

Cont'd 

5-   <u>Help Arrives</u>

I hear Tom's voice while I am putting out some hay for my animals, a chore that doesn't overtax my body or my mind, like him with his staple vegetables.

'Have you cooled down – not still angry with me? You said I wasn't behaving as usual and I was trying your patience. I'd like to say you weren't your normal self either.'

'Fair enough. That night spent chained to the tree took a lot more out of me than I thought. I knew I felt tired, but I was buggered. I slept for 10 hours straight! I don't think I've ever done that before. Maybe I'm older than I think I am, or maybe being close to Robert has added years to my age. I apologise for yesterday.'

We shake hands.

'Are you free now to go to town? I've lined up a meeting with three Elders and this morning's okay for them.'

'Just give me a hand to spread out the last of this hay and mind you don't get bowled over by the young steers – they know not to try that with me now, but you'd be fair game.'

We walk along and kick around what we should tell the Elders. By the time we reach the outskirts of Mole Creek, we feel comfortable. As sure as Hell, we don't want them to reject our request for help.

The Elders, two men and a woman, are seated in the front room of a house and drinking herb tea. They are known to us. One man had been in an older class when I began school, but this was the first time we'd approached them seeking assistance and, critically, not just for help in our Clan territory; the *whole island* is now our focus.

Tom began and did a good job of describing what we'd run into at Brumby's Creek. I butted in to tell them what Robert had said when he and Wayne released me from the bloody chain – "We are well organised and we have plans for this island" – and I add, 'as I understand our law, that's treason, isn't it?'

'It *would* be treason if this bloke Robert is caught *with others*,' the woman says. 'If they are trying to reinstate the Restless culture here: collusion is an essential step. We can't charge an individual for *wanting* that culture to return, but getting together with like-minded people to achieve the return *is* a crime.'

'That's why Tom and I need your help. We came home from Brumby's Creek firm in the belief that Robert *does* have the intention of restoring the Restless culture to our island and that he has a well-disciplined gang to help him.'

'Yes, Ned and I reckon he must have more than the 25 or so who we saw; there were no women there, so he must have other hide-outs too. We just don't know how many or where these are located.'

'We guess that most of Robert's gang reside outside our territory. Also, we suspect he intends to mount an attack on the Assembly at Campbell Town, timed for a full meeting of the Members.'

'Ned and I would like you to arrange two things. First, seek volunteers to be sentries outside the Assembly for maybe a week or so. We surmise Robert intends to strike soon. Secondly, while we believe all the Members must be made aware of the situation, it would be risky for this to be done in the usual way. Far better would be if Elders in other Clan territories could be briefed by you so that they could brief their Members *without* the need to convene in Campbell Town.

'Finally, do you know anyone or any family that may have an amateur radio set-up? If amateur radio enthusiasts are active elsewhere in the world, Robert might already be in contact with other like-minded people.'

We depart with a strong assurance that our needs are understandable, critical for our island's future, and that our requests are plausible to implement.

Cont'd →

6-   <u>Kinjo's Adventure Begins</u>

At this point, I feel I need to hand the story-
telling task over to young Kinjo Yaxley for a
while. I met Kinjo much later on when he played
a very direct role in helping Tom and me, so
I think it proper that he has an opportunity
to explain how he got involved, from when he
volunteered to be a sentry at Campbell Town.
Here's his explanation.

June 1: I ride into Campbell Town and head for the main stables.
Dad had told me to leave his horse there, as it wouldn't be long
before another traveller wanted to head north and Pepper would
get back to our own stables without much delay. I walk along
the streets towards the Assembly. I'd been told the main building
was 300 years old! It's not as big as I had imagined and – to be
honest – neither is Campbell Town. Capital, yes: City, no!

I register my name at the front of the building and am
told to approach a man coming towards me from under a tree.
The man speaks when he gets close.

'Mm - what's your name?'

'Kinjo, and yours?'

'I'm Tim. Kinjo – is that - mm - short for something?'

'In a way. I'm called that after my four grandparents;
Kath and Ian Newitt, my Mum's parents, and June and Ozzi,
Dad's parents. So, I'm Kinjo Yaxley.'

'I - mm - guess islanders in your area - mm - had a problem to find a nickname out of that.'

'Not at all! I've no idea if my parents chose my name to
block the custom for nicknames here, but the kids at school had
no difficulty. From my first day of school, I was called simply
"K".'

'Come far on that horse of yours did you?'

'Not far; Deloraine's where I go to school.'

'Mm - a bit young for this caper, aren't you?'

'I aim to finish school when this task is over, although I'm not sure how long for, because my girlfriend, Lulo Beneventi, keeps urging me to get a job. She says her parents will not let her marry me until I do have work.'

'Beneventi - mm - sounds Italian.'

'Yes, her great grandparents came to our island only ten years or so before the collapse. She's nice and she's clever. She left school a few months ago and already has a good job with some responsibility, because of her ability with numbers. Are you from Campbell Town?'

'From Ross. That's - mm - near enough, I'd say. Been there all my life.'

'Yeah, easy walking distance isn't it? Reckon we'll be here long?'

We've reached the end of the block housing the Assembly, so we turn around and begin walking back.

'Dunno, Kinjo. I suppose - mm - we'll get marching orders sometime. For now, we're to help guard the - mm - Assembly Room. Mm - have you seen a Restless one?'

'Not that I know of, but Ned Youd and Tom Badcock live in my Clan territory and they seem to find it easy.'

'Yeah, those two have quite a reputation. I'm told we should - mm - look out for groups of men that act strange; I gather it's not - mm - easy to recognise someone on his own - mm - as a Restless one. What's your father do?'

'Dad and his brother work together. Dad has a stable and horses for hire and a paddock where people can agist their horses. My uncle runs the smithy next door. I'll probably work there when I leave school, if I don't find a better option. I'd prefer to have a job that will exercise my brain more than just find myself wielding a hammer.'

'Sheep farming's in my blood. I've two boys who help me, so - mm - that's how I can take the time to come here. Know much about your ancestors?'

'Wow, you ask a lot of questions!'

'Got to - mm - pass the time somehow. Sentry duty's boring and I - mm - talk to stay awake.'

We reach the other end of the sentry's beat, so we stop a while and I think how much I know about my ancestors.

'OK. As far as I know, Tim, both sides of my family, the Newitt's and the Yaxley's, arrived here as convicts around 320 years ago. They weren't impressed by those in authority – the Restless culture was in plain view, I suppose – so as soon as they could, they went bush. They vanished, just like hundreds of other convicts did. Fortunately, it was quite easy to carve out a farm and survive in those days and it would be invisible unless you stumbled on it. They were self-sufficient and did not like anyone telling them what to do. I reckon they and all the other convicts like them created our island's culture. The Industrial Revolution was not for them!'

'Our - mm - island was too remote. That - mm - revolution never did make it this far.'

'Lulo and I were saying just that recently. Remote in distance, but more importantly, I reckon, mentally. The rest of the world did not know the island existed or did not want to know what was here; their ignorance was our salvation a century ago.'

Tim continues walking, lost in thought for a few moments.

'I hadn't thought of it that way, but - mm - you've got a good point, yes. If the rest of the world had known - mm - that we would escape the chaos, it would be - mm - standing room everywhere on our island now.'

'Here's a question for you, Tim. We're supposed to look out for suspicious men, but where are the women? The Restless culture is a *mental* attitude, not a physical behaviour.'

'I hadn't - mm - thought of it that way, but it is worth - mm - thinking about. Seems like your girlfriend - mm - has you under her thumb already! My wife bosses me around - mm - that's a reason why I volunteered for sentry duty, to get some peace and quiet. Yeah, a man and a woman, a couple, would be - mm - less suspicious than two men. I'll keep that in mind.'

7-   <u>**A Door Cracks Open**</u>

It's a glorious late autumn morning; soon, winter will be upon us, but today is a day to be out and about. Tom had hired two horses from the Yaxley's – our own are more suited to ploughing. If we were heading in the right direction, we knew not, but the search had to start somewhere. Tom had argued, 'the western part of our territory has been overlooked by us. It's remote, like Yingina. Let's check it out before we go hunting in other territories.'

We cover the ground at a canter and don't tire the horses. We climb out of the shallow depression known as Nowhere Else and head down through trees to Lake Barrington, upstream of the hydroelectric dam wall. The trees come almost to the water's edge. Not a ripple on the surface. It's a popular spot to visit, I guess, but is anyone living here? We turn to ride north towards the dam wall, but before long, Tom calls out; 'Whoa, Buttercup! Look right, Ned, there's a track heading up the hill. Well-kept too, like those I saw below Brumby's Creek. Let's follow it.'

We dismount and tether our horses. The track continues for about 200m then ends. Something has to be nearby. I turn right, in among trees and boulders. Tom goes left.

'Tom, over here; I've found a cave.'

It's not large. Whoever used it had been gone for two days – three at most; the ashes from a fire are still warm. We cast around for some sign of the occupant. Tom sees it first, a piece of wood with the letters "C21" carved on it.

'Camp 21, do you reckon?'

'Maybe. Keep looking.'

This time, I see it.

'It's another locket, not as nice as the one in Nigel's clock, but there's a note inside, "C18, May 28".'

'Hej! That's yesterday, Ned! Our host could be on his way back right now. Don't leave any trace of us. We'll hide the horses and come back here to spend the night if needs be.'

The afternoon drags on. I guess the cave might not be a permanent home and whoever used it comes here only occasionally. Maybe the person will not return direct from Camp 18, for that was what we interpret is the meaning of "C18". On balance, there is no option but to wait until sometime tomorrow before returning east and heading down to Yingina and adjacent territories. This will be my fourth overnight outdoors among trees in the past two weeks; at least, the trees help keep the ground warm, which is just as well at this time of year.

***

May 30: No sign of anyone yet. Tom goes to tend to the horses, but doesn't get far before running back to where I am sitting. He whispers, 'voices – two people I think.' We can observe a short section of the path. Soon, a man and a woman walk past and head up towards the cave. After a minute, we follow and come face to face with them; they're in the act of leaving the cave.

'G'day. Ned and I are hoping you can tell us where Camp 18 is located.'

'You're so clever, I'm sure you can find the way.'

'No, wait John. You and I are no longer connected with Robert and his Force. He said we two are now islanders. I can tell you how to get there, though I reckon it won't be worth your while to go there now.'

'Alright, Sis. Yes it's true; we belonged to Robert's group. We thought the Restless culture offered an *additional* way to live life, not an alternative way. To us, the islanders' culture has always had one weakness; there is no challenge for the mind, no stimulus. Sure, life here is idyllic. You couldn't want for a better climate, there's little friction between people, one big happy family, as the saying goes, but there has to be something more to life. The island's culture expects you to immerse yourself in a pleasant warm bath *all your life!* It's a culture for older people, say over 60 years of age, but Mary and I are still in our thirties. We've decades ahead of us.'

I'd never heard the island culture described like that. Being 60 now, I could see it would be nice to spend my remaining time in a warm bath instead of chasing my steers around the paddocks in wind and rain.

Mary added, 'That's right. We regarded the Restless culture as the icing on the cake; the incentive to get out of that bath and strive to achieve something new, to challenge ourselves. Of course, we still had to work to have enough to eat, but if that was all we did, you could reason that it was mere subsistence farming.'

I said, 'we'd like to hear more of what you have to say. Maybe our interest in Camp 18 can wait. This cave is too small for all four of us to sit in with any comfort. What's more, we stopped you from going somewhere. I propose we descend to the lake and find a spot to sit down, now the sun is out.'

Tom goes to tend to our horses. We pass by their horses and find a rock to sit on.

'That cave up there; is it just a mailbox for messages from Robert?'

'Two ways – we can leave a message for him too. At least we could until two days ago. We came here today because Mary wanted to retrieve her locket.'

'So, other Restless ones act as mailmen do they?'

'Mail girls too; Robert reckoned a woman wandering through a territory would not seem to be threatening, hence would not attract a lot of attention, while Robert's men could focus on "men's work" as he used to put it.'

'You live near here?'

'Yes, we took over our parents' farm at Nowhere Else when they passed away. Mary and I never married. Our parents were very religious and I think they scared any suitors we might have had.'

'John and I enjoy each other's company, but it would be nice for some external stimulation – mental stimulation – and when we heard of Robert's methods, we made an effort to join. That was three years ago, almost exactly as a matter of fact.'

'Thanks. Tom and I have never inspected the Barrington part of our Clan territory. Not many people live around here, but we thought it worth doing a brief search for Restless ones. Ah, here's Tom. Tom, I reckon I've an answer to why we never saw any women at Brumby's Creek. Robert had sent the women to deliver a message to the outliers of his group to have them come to the meeting at Camp 18.'

'So, you've met Robert?'

'Yes, John. We have a score or two to settle with him, don't we Tom?'

'Ned's right. Ned wet his pants!'

'That's enough Tom. Let's say Robert put me in an awkward situation.'

I didn't want to elaborate further and it would have been better if Tom had kept quiet.

'What happened at the Camp 18 meeting?'

'We went there not knowing the purpose of the meeting. That was normal. Robert's method of mailing information to his group was to never reveal more than the location and date in case the message fell into the wrong hands.'

'Yes, we were a little surprised by how many people there were. These meetings usually took the form of a mutual support gathering, where we could talk of our plans and love of the good things associated with the Restless culture – things we could never say in daily life on the island – but not everyone felt the need for support at any one time, so numbers varied.'

'What did they see as the attractions of the Restless culture?'

'Oh, different things at different times. A theme common

to the various discussions we had, I guess, was planning how to change aspects of life on the island to make it more satisfying.'

'Satisfying to you and them?'

'To them, yes. We enjoyed planning how to make the changes.'

'Did these discussions require islanders, not at Robert's meetings, to change what they wanted to do?'

'Well, often this was the case. We live on our farm, but many of those we talked with were town dwellers and they often bemoaned the lack of progress there. I gather many towns don't have an organised garbage collection, or perhaps there is no communal effort to tidy up the streets – no flower beds beside footpaths, etc..'

What they were saying was accurate to a point; the key was to understand *why* towns could appear untidy. Tom spoke. 'I could debate the need for a communal effort. Our island culture doesn't require that the streets be dirty or uncared for. Our culture emphasises personal choice. One person may choose to keep a tidy house and surrounds while another person might not care a damn about such matters. By contrast, the Restless culture required communal town councils everywhere and regulations were imposed on these. That's the difference! One culture places personal choice on a pedestal, while the other stomped on personal choice with its boots on. Ned and I travel a lot and we see some towns where the residents volunteer time to look after parts of their town in addition to their own home.'

'Tom's right. Town councils were done away with when the Restless culture collapsed. Councils were a form of remote control and that is detested by us islanders – look where it got the rest of the world! What happened at Camp 18?'

'Robert called the meeting to order and said we represented the Force – capital "F" – of people he planned to lead in a campaign to re-establish the Restless culture on the island. He then told anyone who was not prepared to stay with the campaign all the way to the end to leave.'

Tom glances at me; this is real news! Mary continued.

'I was uncomfortable with this plan. We told you before that we did not see the Restless culture as the *only* culture. We would have preferred to find a way for both cultures to co-exist in some way, but I thought it was certain that Robert's plan was not going to achieve that, so I started to walk out and John followed me. What would you say, John – there might have been about sixty persons left at the meeting?'

'Yeah, that would be about right. We've no idea what Robert's plan was; he did not want us deserters to know.'

'Do you know Robert's real name?'

'No, he was just Robert to us.'

'How would you describe his character?'

'Rather aloof. I would say he is quite clever, but he is careful to maintain a distance between himself and the group. He might be a successful leader if his plans are shown to be good ones – you know, "success breeds success" – but his personality wouldn't inspire many.'

'Yes, Mary's right.'

'Ned and I would agree, wouldn't we?'

I nodded, 'he showed me that he had no sympathy for "non-believers". That was his deliberate intention. He says "please" and "thank you" to indicate a gentle nature to his supporters, but I wonder if they are taken in by that.'

'Yeah, good question.'

'What about Nigel and Wayne?'

'Nigel is Robert's son and does what he is told. Wayne is a mystery to me; he seems to be in Robert's good books but I am not sure why.'

'Do you know where they live? Do you know where many of the people at Robert's meetings lived?'

'No. Robert was quite definite; he said it would be hard for any of us to live an individual life if we knew where others lived – the temptation to socialise would be strong and as soon as we came together, the risk was high that islanders would detect our cultural interests.'

'We recognised his point of view was for our benefit.'

I reckon we have gained about as much as we are likely to get and it is time to let John and Mary get back to their farm.

'Tom and I will head south-east now. Can you suggest any places where we can locate Restless ones or where Robert might be planning to show his hand?'

Mary said, 'I'm guessing, but I'd think you should try and find where residents of the old capital went when the Restless culture collapsed. These had to move out to find food, you know. Robert's key supporters are almost certain to be descended from those people – the resentment of losing their former "status" in island life could have been passed on.'

'*Shit!* Sorry, Mary, for swearing. I was addressing Ned. He and I never thought of that. It could be that Robert's plan is based on occupying the old capital, not Campbell Town. That would appeal to the people you've mentioned.'

'You've given us a lot to think about and we thank you', I said. 'Until now, the two of you have had an isolated life, but your sole window to a wider world has closed, so I urge you to get involved with a few islanders' groups, there are plenty to choose from. You'll find one or two that *do* present a cause to get you out of that bath each day.'

Tom nods, 'I'm a farmer, but I studied woodworking and I get a lot of enjoyment from making wooden objects that other people are happy to buy from me. Cast around and something will take your fancy. If you come to Mole Creek, ask after us; Ned and I'd love to introduce you to the islanders we know.'

***

Tom and I converse on the way home. 'They were nice kids and they meant well; they're best out of the Restless culture.'

'Yes, Ned, but I could throttle their parents. My guess is that they chose to farm at Nowhere Else, because it is so isolated, hence they could bring up their kids free of contamination by us heathens. John and Mary will be hard pressed to sell their farm and it might not be easy for them to become accepted into another Clan.'

'Weird religious sects once abounded on the island.'

'Some can be found today too, Ned. Bill Yaxley told me that his young Kinjo is a Buddhist. From what I've heard, Buddhists seem to be tolerant of others, but some religions would seem to combine well with the Restless culture; the intolerance towards anyone who did not share your particular religion matches the intolerance of advocates of the Restless culture to anyone who was not a wholehearted supporter of that culture.'

We halt at a creek to let our horses drink.

'Where's the most likely place for us to find Robert's key supporters?'

'The Coal Valley would be a good bet, Ned. The soil is good and the irrigation system was installed before 2050. There would have been many established landholders already there at the collapse, so those fleeing the old city would have had to fight for a foothold or two, unless they had some money with them. East of the city there was more open land, but I suppose it is still open, because it lies in a rain shadow, maybe the soil is not as good and irrigation was never introduced.'

'Tom, we also need to understand how Robert intends to occupy the city. He hasn't many followers, so he'll need to focus on just a few key targets, like the commandos did during the Second World War; they'd head to power stations, oil storage tanks, train stations, etc.. In Robert's case, he would want to *control* these, not destroy them.'

'Makes sense.'

'And symbols of the Restless culture's power base could be on his list. Let's compare ideas tomorrow. We'll need to visit the Elders again, have them move the sentries from Campbell Town and find more men to support us in a campaign further south.'

Cont'd →

8-   <u>The Counter-Plan</u>

We sit facing the same three Elders.

'Tom and I came upon two young people yesterday who were kicked out of Robert's group when they decided his plans were not to their liking.' I turned to Tom.

'That's right. They told Ned and me of a meeting at a place called Camp 18 on 28 May. We don't know where that is, but about 60 people stayed to hear Robert's plan for how he intends to *restore* the Restless culture to our island. He called the group his Force – force with a capital F. Because the two we met showed they were unwilling to go the whole way with his campaign, Robert withheld all details until they were well out of earshot.

'Ned and I accept what these two could tell us and we think we – and you – need to revise our plans. Thus, it is more probable now that Robert's target is not Campbell Town, but the old capital. This core group of supporters are not many and it is plausible that their parents or grandparents were influential people in the city up until the collapse. The descendants of such people would be attracted to a plan that saw them re-establishing their "place" in the city. There could be other, less fanatical Restless ones on the island who would support the Force once they'd seen that Robert had regained control of key parts of the city.'

I can see the Elders are thinking about this possibility. It does require more than a momentary thought to grasp that the old city could have a relevance to some people, even though the majority of islanders give it no value at all. We never refer to it by name.

I take over from Tom. 'We're here to ask you to help organise for a fighting force of two hundred or more islanders to protect some areas of the city and have them there in the next few days. If Robert succeeds in his initial plan he will gain credibility and it will be much harder to defeat his Force later on. Apart from a half-dozen or so of the Campbell Town sentries, the rest should go south, but we will need extra forces as well. When could you get action from the other Clans do you think?'

The Elders look at each other. Eventually, one of the men speaks.

'We should focus on territories closer to the city, to shorten the travel time. Your influence will be important too, so you could visit a couple of Clans and we can provide you with our authority. To be honest, though, I doubt we could get 200 people into the city in less than a week. I believe it is necessary to call all our Members to an Assembly to have them approve this campaign as official; an All-Island Defence of Our Culture is what is called for, I reckon. I am not saying this must take place first, but we should set things in train now.'

The other Elders nod in support and the female Elder says, 'leave it to me.'

'Tom and I have grappled with the task of devising the most effective defence, given our limitations in time and numbers. We surmise that most members of Robert's Force will approach the city from the north, rather than the south and that very few of its members already live in the city. Hence, we should block all three bridges that could come into play, as well as the road along the south bank of the Derwent River.'

'Whichever way Ned and I look at it, any plan of ours will have several weaknesses. The first one, and it's a serious weakness, is that it will become apparent to anyone involved in Robert's Force that we islanders are on the hunt. This can't be helped; it's a part of our culture to spread the word of what we are doing willy-nilly and the word is bound to reach Restless ones in every territory. To counter this, we should give everyone who joins us *two* stories; one is to be the correct destination for that person plus the duty we foresee when he or she gets there, and a second story is to be about a different destination. It is that second story we would encourage our people to talk about while pleading for them not to talk about the first story. Of course, both stories are bound to get to Robert and we can just hope that he is confused about what our real plan is.'

I continued, 'we suggest that the other story should be that we believe the Restless ones intend to occupy Port Arthur in Premadena territory. Islanders consider Port Arthur to be our premier cultural centre, because of the vivid, well-documented history there of the cruel treatment of convicts by the authorities, who were the ancestors of today's Restless ones in our minds. Hence, we think it would be a dramatic demonstration of Robert's power and determination if he was to take Port Arthur back under *his* control; of course, we intend to be aggressive defenders.'

I see each Elder nod and lean forward. We have their full attention now!

'We should sound keen to trap his Force on the peninsula south of Eaglehawk Neck, the place where 300 years ago the authorities maintained a line of soldiers and dogs to stop convicts – our ancestors – escaping from Port Arthur. Thus, we should ask the elders of Premadena territory to arrange for some men to assemble at Eaglehawk Neck.'

Tom spoke up. 'The supposed destination of Port Arthur is advantageous to us, because any of our troops heading south towards the original city are *equally* on their way to Port Arthur, because the route to the latter diverges when you are on the outskirts of the city.'

'The second weakness Tom and I foresee may be harder to overcome. It is probable that the members of the Force will make their way to their designated targets as individuals – at most in pairs (e.g., a man and a woman) – and this will make it hard to detect them. It would help if Robert's plan requires each one to reach their target on the same day, thus there might be a surge in foot traffic across the bridges before that date. We can't pin all our hopes on this, so we need to have an extra duty for our sentries.

'We believe that each traveller approaching the city has to be considered an enemy; the reason for entering the city needs to be convincing for him to pass through. Our sentries are to suggest to *each* one that he should return home and come back in a week or two's time. Here, our culture will be beneficial, because it is not in our nature ever to be punctual, while a Restless one is forever conscious of time passing. If a sentry's request fails to deter a person, one of our troops would accompany the person – "escort them" – to whichever destination they claim to be heading for. After an hour or so, it could become apparent if the person has an ulterior motive or not; if not, the escort would return to his sentry duty. If the former, he should continue all the way to the target. With luck, most of Robert's men who reach their targets will do so in presence of an equal number of our "escorts" and Robert's plan will have lost its surprise element.'

I sense that we have the support we need.

Tom says we have one more request. 'Each Clan has its own constabulary. Of course, these do talk across territory borders, but their real value now lies in their pretty intimate knowledge of their Clan's fellow citizens. To the extent constables could be spared, it would be a great help if they could stand beside our sentries and hear the stories provided in answer to a sentry's query. Of course, our close-knit community means most people are known to a great many others, sometimes via mutual acquaintances, but we feel it is best not to rely on a sentry from one territory being familiar with any person referred to by a traveller from another territory.'

9-   **<u>Kinjo on Alert at the Bridge</u>**

Back to Kinjo and his experiences for a while.

Tim and I volunteered to go south to take up duty at Bridgewater. Tim brought with him a simple map, which he collected from his farm, showing the locations of suburbs in the old capital, and we often looked at it as we walked along. I gained a good awareness of the geography of the place.

Until 100 years ago, the bridge at Bridgewater had been used by cars, trucks and trains and one section of the bridge could be raised to let ships pass through. For some reason known to them alone, a large flock of black swans could always be found on the river within spitting distance of the causeway linking the bridge to the southern bank of the river, where it joined up with the road from the western part of the island, which ran along the south bank. Today, the bridge sees foot and horse-drawn traffic.

We are among the few sentries at the northern end of the bridge, while a larger group is stationed at the confluence of the causeway and the river road. The two sentry posts are just over one kilometre apart and communication can be achieved by semaphoring.

'This is - mm - better than Campbell Town, don't you think? To - mm - pass the time we can try our luck fishing.'

'That's my favourite pastime, Tim. I reckon there's nothing better than a feed of fresh fish.'

'Yeah, I've - mm - noticed that you eat meat, but aren't - mm - Buddhists vegetarian?'

'It depends how deep you choose to follow the religious dogma. My interest is more focused on the Buddhist view of human relationships. An important point about Buddha's teachings is control of your own mind. Keep your mind from greed, and your behaviour will be right, your mind pure, and you can avoid all evils. It is a man's own mind, not his enemy that lures him into evil ways.'

'Okay, but what will you - mm - do if a Restless one tries to pass over the bridge?'

'I suspect it will not be easy to identify him as a Restless one, so I will speak with respect and without trying to threaten him. It is the stranger's mind that determines if he is a Restless one or not, hence I will attempt to understand how his mind works and lead him to see how the Restless culture is too toxic to be allowed a foothold on our island. I see this approach being valid whether or not he is a Restless one.'

Tim stood quietly for a while before replying.

'I'm - mm - not convinced. Let's say we take it in turns - mm - to deal with people wanting to cross the bridge.'

'Alright, but remember; we are islanders and our culture is to not force our desires on another person, so you can't physically block that person's access to the bridge – if you do, you are acting as if *you* were a Restless one. No offence meant, Tim, but if your sheep could talk, wouldn't it be interesting to hear how they view your approach as their farmer?'

'Baaaa!'

A man was approaching from the north. Tim tosses a coin and I get a chance to demonstrate my theory.

'G'day, I'm Kinjo. Going far are you?'

'Naa, just to Claremont.'

'That's about an hour away, isn't it? Do you live there?'

'No. My mother does, if you must know.'

'Come this way often then, do you?'

'As a matter of fact, I do. I bring food with me for my mother. But, what's with this welcoming committee of yours? Those four blokes leaning on the bridge railing don't appear to be fishing.'

'There's a rumour that a gang of Restless ones plans to

capture part of the old capital. Their culture is toxic and we can't allow them to succeed. We'd much prefer that you delay your visit for a week or so, while we check out this rumour.'

'But, I'm not one of them,'

'Where did you come from?'

'Near Tunbridge.'

'Gee, that's almost 100 km. Won't your Mum move closer to you?'

One of the men leaning on the railing calls out, 'Tunbridge you say. Do you know Bill Henderson?'

'Not directly, but I played football with his brother a few times.'

'Well, are you going to delay your visit like I suggested?'

'No. It would be too much trouble and I'm innocent.'

'Okay, I am going to keep you company. Let's go. What did your father do?'

'For a long time, my parents ran what was the Main Café in Claremont. Of course, that had been a much more prosperous place prior to the collapse, but my parents eked out a living by trying to provide the dwindling number of nearby residents, women in the main, with whatever they needed – sort of general store like. We were fortunate to have a house with a large backyard and a good-sized front lawn, both of which we converted into beds for vegetables. Mum planted flowers for borders and she sold these at the shop – an easy money-earner they were. We got used to bartering.'

'Did you have access to meat, or were you always vegetarian?'

'We became pseudo-vegetarians as a consequence of the collapse. If someone had meat or fish for sale, we'd take it, though to be honest we got to the point sometimes where we'd trade or on-sell the meat in our café rather than eat it ourselves.'

While we head over the causeway, one of the men on the bridge signals to the main group of sentries gathered on the south bank:

SUSPECT SAYS FROM TUNBRIDGE VISITING MOTHER AT CLAREMONT

At the south bank, I say, 'Wait here for a minute or two' and I go to talk with the group of sentries.

'Says he doesn't know Bill Henderson of Tunbridge, but played football with his brother – can anyone verify this? I believe he's one of us, but best is for one of you to go to Claremont with him to confirm his innocence. Is anyone here familiar with Claremont? You'll be back in two hours. Ok?'

As I shake hands with the stranger, I realise that I don't know his name.

'Before you go, what's your name?'

'Sam.'

'Sam who?'

'Evans. Geez, you blokes are serious, aren't you?'

'We've no choice. Our ancestors endured over two hundred years during which they had to tolerate the imposition of the Restless culture while keeping their own culture hidden from view. We are NOT going to return to that time!'

I arrive back at the bridge just as Tim prepares to deal with the next person to appear from the north. Tim steps forward.

'Restless ones - mm - to the left, islanders to the right.'

'Do I get a prize for guessing correctly?'

'No nonsense. If you - mm - want to go over the bridge, show me - mm - who you are.'

Taking a coin out of his pocket, the man tosses it in the air and looks at how it lands. He goes to the left.

'You're not going - mm - any further till you explain why you're here. First, though, what's - mm - your name?'

'No, first what's your name?'

'Tim.'

'Barrie.'

'That'll - mm - do for now. Why did you come here?'

'I come here once a month when I bring food for my mother.'

'Mm - where does she live?'

'Moonah.'

'Where are you - mm - coming from?'

'Avoca.'

A general murmur of surprise emanates from the cluster of sentries looking on.

'Sheep farmer or - mm - tin miner?'

'Neither, I'm a businessman.'

'In - mm - Avoca? You must - mm - live a lonely life. How many live there apart - mm - from you?'

'The blacksmith and the brewer. I run the pub.'

'You need - mm - a fourth for a game of cards.'

'There's a retired miner. We all think he stumbled upon a gold deposit somewhere – he doesn't say much. He seems to always have cash to spend.'

'So, he's the reason you - mm - blokes *can* live in Avoca!'

'More or less. The Fingal Valley's a nice place to live, you know.'

'Yeah, but so is - mm - the rest of this island – except for the old capital. Moonah's not - mm - grand, so why does your mother - mm - still live there? It must be 150km from Avoca.'

'She's getting on in years and Moonah's where her friends are.'

'Given that you - mm - identified as a Restless one, I can't allow you to - mm - cross the bridge any time in the next two weeks. Not - mm - unless you reveal what part you will play in Robert's plan.'

'Robert who?'

'I'm - mm - tired of playing funny buggers with you. I'll escort you to the south bank of the river.'

'What? Do you think I've come all the way from Avoca just to jump off the causeway and drown myself in the Derwent?'

This ludicrous image generates several guffaws.

'Can't be - mm - too sure of people these days! We're - mm - here to stop a gang of Restless ones taking over the old capital and - mm - subjecting the island to their callous culture again. Is that what you want to see happen?'

'Is that what your bloke Robert is all about?'

'He's *not* "our" bloke – he's - mm - the *leader* of the gang!'

Meanwhile, a message is semaphored across the river: SUSPECT NOMINATED AS RESTLESS ON WAY TO MOONAH

Tim told me later that he said to Barrie at the south bank, 'One of the blokes here will - mm - go with you to your Mum's place. I'd advise you - mm - to tell the bloke everything you know about Robert's plans.' Tim then talked with a sentry before walking back to the bridge. I smile; 'It takes all sorts, doesn't it: innocent or Restless?'

'Dunno. You - mm - mentioned my sheep before. I can tell you, there's - mm - always one of them that's having a bad day – won't do what I want – and I can never pick - mm - which one it's going to be. With those two blokes, the - mm - proof will be revealed at Claremont and at Moonah, I reckon.'

'Yes, we'll have success here only when persons turn back at our request.'

10-   <u>The Town Within the City</u>

I'm back. Kinjo and his mate Tim met some odd characters! When feasible to do so, Tom and I had travelled south using horses to cover the ground in the quickest way. I went to Premadena and Tom went to Trayapana, two Clan territories east of the old city. After talking to Elders there, we joined up and crossed the river by the southernmost of the three bridges.

June 6:

Neither of us has been in the old capital for about forty years. As best I can recall, it has not changed much; a few more houses and buildings have fallen down and the streets are greener now, the weeds destroying more of what had been bitumen.

It does not present as an attractive destination, though that had sometimes been the view even before the collapse. I am always amused when I recall the words attributed to a once-prominent businessman who lived in the old "could-a-been", rival capital in the north of the island. Referring to the actual capital in the south, he had said, "If it wasn't for the zinc works and the Government payrolls, it would be a nice place for a seaside village."

Tom interrupts my thoughts. 'What say, which of Robert's possible targets should we head for?'

'I'm not sure it matters, Tom. We've a list of four, but each one is guesswork on our part. So, let's head to the nearest one. If all's quiet there, we can move to the next.'

'Fair enough. You and I have one definite advantage over all the other islanders who are helping us. We have met maybe half the members of Robert's Force, so with luck we'll be able to recognise them for who they are.'

'And, they'll recognise us! I think we need to be cautious in going around corners. Imagine that *we* are commandos too!'

For once, I think I've out-thought him. Tom hesitates when he comes to the next corner, peers around the building, then walks straight across. This momentary hesitation doesn't influence his talking; that continues uninterrupted.

'I doubt they are armed with guns, or if they do have guns, they'd be relying on ammunition that would be over 100 years old; would this still work when the trigger is pulled and how many bullets would they have anyway?'

'They'd need just two to deal with us, so don't behave like Superman, Tom. Leave that job to me.'

Tom is silent at the next corner, but not for long.

'Alright, I'll stand behind you.'

'Good. I'll break wind for you.'

'Ned! The expression is "I'll break *the* wind for you"!'

'No, I meant it the way I said it.'

We've come close to the one-time Parliament House. The lawns out front have been cleared of trees and the ground is now somebody's vegetable patch. There's nobody in sight. A cold southerly breeze blows in from the nearby waterfront, where once upon a time an assortment of ships and small boats would have been moored. Is this building on Robert's list? Symbolic, but not Robert's first objective, I suspect.

'It might be a race, Tom. If we're lucky, the troops we've asked Premadena and Trayapana territories to send will be able to surround the building before Robert's Force gets here. I suggest we make our way to the next place on our list.'

For 250 years, the city would have been teeming with life; human beings in every building, on every street – movement in all directions. So far today, we have not seen anybody else. We aren't sure where members of the Force might be lurking and anyone we might bump into could be a friend or a foe.

We have to be on guard, unsure whether we have already been observed by a member of Robert's gang, perhaps by Robert himself.

Another symbolic building is Government House. Surely this would be on Robert's list! It is large and it could house everyone in his Force, yet until the collapse, it was the official domicile of one person, the island's Governor.

Located on a hill with a good view in most directions and surrounded by extensive lawns and gardens, we'd been told that Government House had been "reclaimed" by islanders soon after the collapse. At the bottom of the hill there would be easy access to the river for fishing.

We start to climb. The hill – known as The Domain – was potentially the *sole* place in the old capital capable of providing food for a town's worth of people. I notice that the land on the Domain has been converted into fields with space for several cows and sheep allowed to roam there as well. Might the people here be unwilling to allow Robert to muscle his way in? Perhaps we can recruit more troops to help our cause.

Together we work our way in between vegetable beds. This time of year would be a quiet time for these farmers as well. How would they be spending the time?

A brief movement, Tom has seen it too. Someone is walking on the roof of the House. A watchman or a worker? It would be a good time to undertake any roof repairs prior to the winter. If a watchman, it seems that we do not present a threat, or is he a poor choice as observer?

We are soon on the level ground in front of this imposing building. The massive doors are open. We step in, our ears greeted by the sounds of children having fun further along the corridor.

'Hullo, is anyone home?'

Tom's voice brings a result. A door opens and a woman steps into the hall. A woman in her sixties, I think.

'Hullo, I'm Ned Youd and this is my mate Tom Badcock. We're from up north. We're looking for Restless ones.'

'There aren't any here, but my son will be glad to know. He's gone fishing, but he'll be back soon. My husband's working on the roof.'

I continue, 'Is your family the only one here?'

'*Lordy no!* There are 120 people here. Twenty families, some with three generations like my family. It's one building, but we are spread out pretty well. The grand reception room has been partitioned by walls and is now a home for one family of seven.'

'But, where is everyone?'

'Oh, here and there. This is not like a commune, with everybody in everyone else's pockets. Here, we live as if we were in a town. Most of us have ancestors who lived in the country. So, you see, we each have a "house" in this building and the farm on the hill is divided into family plots too.'

Tom is quick to ask, 'But, where's the pub? A town is not a town without one!'

'Just to the north of here used to be the Botanical Gardens with the Keeper's Lodge. That's the pub.'

I persist, 'I'm still wondering where the people are right now. We've seen you and your husband and we've heard the kids further along. They can't all be fishing are they?'

'I suppose you came here from down near the city centre', the woman says. 'That's an area of little interest to us; really it's useless. We spend most of our free time now at the end of autumn fossicking in the suburbs north and west of the city centre where there are lots of houses, some with gardens and places where we can grow things and there are fruit trees too.'

'Ned and I were just at Parliament House. We saw nobody, but it looks as if somebody lives there.'

'Yes, the Bourke's; a big family, they need most of the open space nearby just to support themselves.'

This is an intriguing story, but one thing does puzzle me.

'If the families here were country people, then why establish a life here after the collapse?'

'There was a huge exodus from the city into the adjacent countryside where people like my great grandparents had been living all their life. The city people were desperate and they brought their city arrogance with them. Many of the islanders resisted, of course, but our culture led some of us to decide to move someplace else. A few figured there must be space back in the city and my great grandparents headed straight for Government House. They were the first to do so; that's why I now live nearest the entrance. My grandparents worked hard to turn the lawns into vegetable gardens and it was a difficult time for them, but others followed and after some time it all came together as you see it now.'

We wait at the House to talk with the woman's son, or to her husband, whichever man arrives first. The wait is unsettling as we want to inspect the other sites on our list and any delay on our part could put us at a disadvantage. The one consolation would be if the townspeople at the House can lend us valuable support.

Not long after noon, the son comes back with five fish and a minute or two later his father descends from the roof. Lunchtime calls, and Tom and I are invited to join the family, which we now see also consists of the son's wife and their two girls.

Mrs Weeding senior says, 'Ned and Tom are looking for Restless ones. I said there are none here.' I explain the reason for our search and add, 'I'd be pleased if some of your townspeople could assist. Tom and I are convinced this bloke Robert, whoever he is in real life, means business, but his Force is small in numbers and our best chance of success is to show that his plan isn't going to work before he can claim a success or two.'

The son, George, responds, 'I'm sure quite a few of us

could help you. Our farm work will recommence in about ten days, so most of us have spare time right now and we have good reason to resist a return of the Restless culture. The people who forced our ancestors from their farms a century ago were Restless ones – no doubt about it. They saw their own need; country people were non-people in their eyes.'

George offers to call a meeting of the residents of the House that evening and I suggest a few ways by which I think their assistance could be of good value. 'One of us will return early tomorrow to assign various roles to any volunteers.'

Mr Weeding senior asks us to describe this Robert bloke. We do our best, adding that, while he feigns politeness, he is quite ruthless. Mr Weeding says, 'I have met a man – Dick Loone – who could fit that description to some extent, though I would hesitate to bet on it being the *same* bloke. It's a good ten years since he arrived here and introduced himself. I've always remembered his name; it's unusual, don't you agree? He asked if we wanted to return to the country and I said we were quite comfortable here. He went away and I've never seen him since. He didn't say where he was from and I didn't think to ask, because his suggestion that we move back was of no interest. You know, as long as the city was the capital, with all the negative things that title brought with it, I would not have thought of settling here, but in its present state, the former capital is a pretty good place to call home. I don't want this neighbourhood ruined now by Restless ones.'

We give them descriptions of Nigel and Wayne as well before we depart. We head down the hill from Government House and manage to spy the lie of the land at the two locations that we thought could be on Robert's list. All is quiet and we lack manpower resources to maintain a watch over these places.

We find an empty house still in a good condition and spend the night there – much better than sleeping yet another night under the trees somewhere.

11-   <u>Bridge Duty Escalates</u>

Much later, Kinjo told me of one key break-
through at Bridgewater on June 8. Here's
his recollection of what happened.

After three days, Tim and I considered ourselves seasoned
Bridgewater sentries and the fishing *was* good! There was
something akin to a daily pattern; between five and ten individuals would arrive intending to cross the river and two or three
would heed the advice to turn back and wait a couple of weeks.
The rest were escorted to the south bank of the river, their reasons for wanting to cross the river being plausible – if taken at
face value, as had to be the case if a sentry was to act true to the
island's culture.

On the other hand, the precaution of escorting a person
to their stated destination had been effective. Both Sam Evans
and Barrie were shown thereby to be islanders, but today another traveller began acting strange as he and the escorting sentry
were approaching the stated destination. Had the suspect realised that the sentry was about to be at one of the assembly points
of the Force? The destination had sounded innocuous when the
sentries at the southern end of the causeway heard it mentioned,
but the escort had not tired of the walk and soon would see the
destination for what it was. Was Robert's plan, with its apparent
need for secrecy, about to be wrecked?

The traveller started running and dodging into laneways
and jumping fences to get away from the sentry. The sentry told
us he did his best to follow, until he realised that he was being
led away from what must be a sensitive spot, after which he returned to the causeway as fast as he could to raise the alarm and
to advise us of this likely destination of members of the Force.
He didn't know if he had done the right thing, he said; sentries

were supposed to accompany their suspect all the way to the declared destination, still, this suspect's behaviour had implied that the location *would* play a part in Robert's plan.

The sentries held a meeting and concluded that this particular suspect could have been the first member of the Force to cross the river at Bridgewater and tomorrow might see an attempted influx of Restless ones. The sentries decided to implement a new plan. From tomorrow, all travellers would be held at the south bank sentry post until five or six had been so detained, at which time a group of sentries would escort all potential suspects together to each destination in turn. Along the way, any person thereby proven to be an islander would be released, but all escorts would continue to accompany the remaining suspects.

***

The new day dawns; sentries on the bridge now have to obtain the detailed address of each suspect's destination before allowing the suspect to cross the river.

We do not have to wait long. A couple are seen approaching the bridge; he is tall, she is short for a woman. They look to be in their thirties.

'Good morning, I'm Kinjo. Do you plan to cross the river?'

'Meg and I have that intention, yes, but what's it to you?'

'My friends and I have been asked to control who uses the bridge. There's a rumour that a gang of Restless ones are planning to gather in the old city and we are worried what such a gathering might be for. Where are you headed?'

'Meg's grandparents are buried in Cornelian Bay Cemetery and we pay them a visit every June while we're between farming seasons.'

'Do you come straight back over this bridge afterwards?'

'We may, but we'll decide when we've paid our respects. Last year, we found an empty house and stayed the night; there are lots of empty houses, you know. Who asked you to guard this bridge?'

'We come from different Clans and our Elders asked us to volunteer some time. Like you, some of us are free of farm duties, so it was no problem for us – and the fishing's good here. I've another question; when were Meg's grandparents buried?'

'If you must know, it was after the collapse of the city. Meg's parents are buried in the same cemetery – we made a special effort to reunite the generations, so we can make one trip to tend all her ancestor's graves.'

'So, your wife comes from city stock!'

'Yes, but that doesn't make her a Restless one, does it? Are you going to let us cross?'

'I'd recommend that you postpone your trip for a week or ten days. The grandparents will no doubt still appreciate the effort you're making when you do get there, but it doesn't have to be just this week.'

'That's not for you to judge, young man, and your attempt at humour isn't funny. Let's go, Meg.'

'Not so fast! You can pass over the bridge after you've given me your names and the names of Meg's grandparents.'

'What the Hell for?'

'It's for your safety. If I let you pass, I'm responsible to ensure that you don't get caught up in any fighting that might erupt if this rumour turns out to be true. If you give me your names, our own forces in the city will be able to guide you away from any hot spots – without names; you will automatically be assigned a Restless label!'

Names given, I escort the couple to the south bank, where they are surprised to find a larger group of sentries waiting. As part of the new plan, these sentries had taken the precaution of remaining out of sight of the bridge, save for the man who watches for any semaphored messages. I return to the bridge after passing on all the information I've gathered. The man had said his name was Dave Loone.

Tim smiles, 'Nice - mm - work young man.'

'Thanks. I gave the situation a good deal of thought last night and I hope I covered all bases. Personally, I reckon they are Restless ones with a half-plausible story so I felt it was necessary to obtain Meg's grandparents' names. That information will give the escorting team a solid means to test the truth of their story.'

12-   <u>The Combatants are Sighted</u>

First thing this morning, Tom and I found a location, a wooded, one-time recreation oval in the northern part of Moonah, somewhere near the centre of the zone being monitored by our three clusters of sentries and there I awaited Tom's return from Government House. If we now had some extra volunteers, Tom was to suggest that two of these be asked to keep travelling in opposite directions to visit all three bridges, thereby to keep the many sentries informed of each other's experiences and to ensure that Tom or I are kept up-to-date as well.

Around mid-morning, Tom returns with good news. The families had supported George's call for volunteers. Tom and George agreed that at least six men would act as a defensive force to keep Government House from being overrun by Robert's Force. Between them, the families had four horses and George thought that two women could undertake to fill the communications role, utilising two of the horses. This left a maximum of eight men ready to help us and Tom arranged for them to make their way to where I was stationed, where they will form a group that we can lead wherever we decide to head.

Over the next several hours the men arrive and set up camp. They have an assortment of weapons; hoes, axes, etc.. Harry has a horse and Steve has his dog, a kelpie cross. Bruce carries a whip, which he soon reveals he is quite adept at using.

In mid-afternoon, the first horsewoman arrives with news from all bridge control points. The Bridgewater news is interesting. One suspect had evaded an escorting sentry near Pottery Creek Road in Newtown yesterday and, of eleven persons crossing the river at Bridgewater today, *six* proved to be Restless ones when the escorts accompanying the six to their declared destinations noted that these did not match the purported reasons for the visits.

The big news for Tom and me: Dave Loone was in the group of six – this has to be Nigel, Robert's son! Nigel's purported wife Meg was on her way to her grandparents' graves, but the escorts found that no such graves existed. Nigel maybe thought he had a good story in talking about graves – "Dead men tell no tales" – but he hadn't figured on having to deal with persistent escort sentries.

'Details of our sentry plan have not reached the Force's controllers so far, Ned. We might catch even more Restless ones tomorrow.'

The sentries at the Bowen bridge have yet to detect a Restless one and very few travellers have come that way. The sentries at the third and most southerly bridge had their suspicions raised today by three travellers, but conclusive proof was lacking, because their escorting sentries did not persist in going to the supposed destinations.

I instruct our two intrepid horsewomen to make one return visit to all bridges today, explaining to the sentries at the other two bridges the system now in place at Bridgewater and for all sentries to be on the alert for any man fitting our description of Robert or having the surname of Loone. All efforts are to be made to apprehend this person, I say.

One of the horsewomen told me the Bridgewater sentries were maintaining a watch over the six, who were all insisting of their innocence of the Restless charge. The group is at what used to be Elwick Racecourse, a mere two kilometres north of where I stand. We shall pay them a visit first thing tomorrow; a visit that would call the bluff of these suspects!

Tom says, 'I think each one could hide their allegiance to the Restless culture by maintaining an individual status, so despite them now being encircled by only a few sentries, they might choose not to show their true colours and force an escape. If so, it implies that the time has not yet come when Robert's plan calls for the Force to show its muscle.'

We have yet to see any constabulary. These *would* be helpful to have on hand tomorrow; our force lacks any legal authority to arrest a person, so it will be hard to hold suspects for long.

Before choosing a tree to sleep under, Tom and I discuss today's news. Yesterday's lone suspect had headed further south than any of the others. Could he have a special task? The one place of possible importance we knew of, which lies close to his supposed destination, is the control centre from where the high voltage power distribution system, or much of it, was managed. The sentries had reported his name as Ian Dean. Might this be the man we know as Wayne?

'The others have been heading for places north of that destination, Ned, but close enough to Elwick for the racecourse to be their *real* common goal.'

'I'm in a quandary, Tom, as to how to manage the people we have at the Bowen bridge. That has been a quiet crossing point, which tempts me to bring most or all of them to join us.'

'Maybe, but I wouldn't be surprised if Robert hasn't set up a trap there for you. We know there are maybe fifty members of his Force yet to cross the river. What if he arranged for the advance troops to use the other two bridges to lure us into taking our focus off this middle of the three bridges?'

'Good point. The Bowen bridge joins the south bank near the racecourse, so he could get a large number of his men across in one group using Bowen without bumping into many islanders.'

'Yes, without us twigging to his plan either. Do we take a chance and shift some people from the other bridges to guard the Bowen instead?'

'Alright, that seems worth doing. Everything points to tomorrow being the peak date for the Force to assemble in the old city.'

I ask Harry to ride his horse to Bridgewater and direct half of the total number of sentries to move to the Bowen bridge and I instruct another man to make his way to the southern bridge with the same message.

***

Typical; it *would* rain on what promises to be the day we've been waiting for! We are already wet and we can but hope that Robert's Force is comprised of miserable men too.

I leave one man at our "headquarters" and the rest of us head for Elwick. I ask Tom to try to get as close as he can to the people there without being seen, reminding him, 'Don't forget that you walked past a group at Brumby's Creek without you seeing them, but *they* saw you.' Tom grimaces.

I want Tom to catch Nigel by surprise if he can. There looks to be at least a dozen people, one woman amongst ten or more men, all huddled under the roof (or what remained of one) on a former building which now has just two walls intact to some degree. Tom gets right up to one wall unnoticed. It looks as if our sentries had decided that their duty was to watch the suspects, not to watch for anyone coming from outside the race-course.

As soon as Tom walks into the group, I move forward with my men ready to grab anyone who tries to escape. It seems as if Tom's surprise visit has frozen their thinking, but perhaps the explanation for their passiveness is that they were *expecting* the Force to arrive at the racecourse today, hence they have no reason to *go* anywhere.

The sentries seem relieved to find themselves reinforced by my group. Tom comes to me, all smiles:

'I said to Nigel, "G'day Nige, I notice you're still wearing my clogs. I'd like you to explain to your mates here that I make extra fine clogs" and then I turned to the rest of them under the roof and said, "Nige gave me his clock for that pair of clogs. I reckon he got the worst of the deal because Ned and I are now close to wrecking his father's plan to control the island."'"

I ask Tom to begin pressing the Restless ones to divulge details of Robert's plan, while I take three men and visit the Bowen Bridge. It's a walk of about 1,500 metres, so we are soon with the sentries. There are twenty two men at the south end of the bridge. Unfortunately, there is no suitable hiding place, so if Robert arrives at the other end of the bridge, about 900 metres away, he will be able to see us waiting for him.

I walk across the river to inspect the other group of sentries. Might we be able to combine both groups at this northern end and achieve a surprise for anyone intending to use the bridge today? Unfortunately, the other side is also barren with no obvious hiding place for sentries who, if massed here will total almost thirty five men. At that moment, another six men come from the southern bridge and it is obvious that I now control a substantial force willing to defend the island culture. I must not squander this advantage. I decide to withdraw all men to the racecourse, where they can be dispersed in such a fashion as to ensure that anyone who enters the course will not be able to get out, at least without a real fight.

Of course, it is possible Robert's plan was quite different and right now he could be marching on the south side of the river at the head of his Force – a classic bluff!

We can watch and wait – that's all. If all goes well, we'll have a good chance of gaining the upper hand; if not, then we will find ourselves out-foxed with an uphill battle before we can destroy his plan.

I explain all this to Tom. His captives are still passive, which would be unlikely if Robert's plan was not something like we had surmised.

'Maybe, Ned, but what if this group of six are decoys, sent by Robert to fool us into watching them, rather than keeping our eyes on the lookout elsewhere? Nigel was a decoy that caught us.'

'Fair enough, but we are committed right now to controlling the racecourse. It's a gamble, but one I'm comfortable with, at least for the remainder of today.'

It will soon be noon. Helen arrives on her horse after being told of our whereabouts by the man I'd left in north Moonah. She reveals that all was quiet at the other bridges. Nobody had crossed the river so far today. I explain to her that we no longer have sentries at Bowen and she should omit to call at that bridge on her communication round.

I ask Harry to ride to a spot from where he can observe the Bowen without being conspicuous to anyone coming over the bridge. He is to return to the Racecourse if he sees any group of people approaching.

Another wait! For once, I wish I was Robert – *he* knows what his Force is doing, and would be doing too, if all goes to his plan.

I had avoided talking with Nigel or the other Restless ones. Tom had exhausted all the ways he could think of to have them reveal any aspects of Robert's plan. Even Nigel continues to maintain that he knew of no such plan. What more could I do, other than bang some heads together?

We spend time identifying positions and duties for each man under our control. We will have to wait, prepared for the Force to arrive from *any* direction. A small stand of trees at the western end of the course provides a screen for four men I place there in case the Force crosses the river at Bridgewater and the remnants of several stables at the eastern end offers good cover for the main body of my troops, as the Force will have to pass right by these buildings if they have crossed at the Bowen. I try not to contemplate what we'll do if *nobody* arrives today!

The second horsewoman arrives. Jean had visited the bridges in reverse order to Helen. Nothing of note had happened. It is now mid-afternoon; is my hunch correct or have I guessed the wrong day – will it be *tomorrow*? If so, I'll soon have to set about finding food for all the islanders at the racecourse. One curious thing is that our captives had brought food with them and some of the food remains. Had they been told to expect a longer wait at Elwick than the day they've spent so far under the watch of our sentries?

I ask Jean to alert the families at Government House that we could use their help with food.

The one bright spot; the rain stopped soon after noon and at times there is blue sky visible between the clouds. A few smiles start to appear on our faces as well.

Harry rides into the course and dismounts. He's seen a group of men, about thirty he thinks, approaching the far end of the Bowen Bridge. Did this mean Robert had split his Force into two divisions, or is the smaller number than we'd anticipated an indication that some of his troops have got cold feet? Perhaps the rain had dampened their enthusiasm, and is the arrival of Robert's troops late in the day also a sign of problems with the Force? Tom brings my thoughts back to the present; we have around half an hour to get ready.

[I later learned that Kinjo and his mate Tim had been in the group of sentries I took from Bowen to Elwick and Kinjo later recalled for me their experience while hiding in the stables:

'Late in the afternoon, I saw a solitary horse and rider go past the stables and head to the main course building. Tim had said, "I think Restless ones would - mm - tend to have been pencil pushers – those with shiny trouser bums, because it would - mm - be in their nature to tell others what to do, not to - mm - get their hands into dirty work like brawling and bar fights. I suspect their - mm - descendants now marching here would aspire to being - mm - managers too, not workers."

'It wasn't long before the Force came into view. They weren't in a marching formation, but rather they resembled a crowd departing after a football game – twos here, threes there, and strung out along the road from the bridge. Tim counted thirty two, but wasn't sure if the last of them had come into view.

He didn't detect anyone in charge – surely they would have a leader! He whispered; "I - mm - could do with my sheepdogs! They'd soon have this - mm - mob hemmed in a circle.""]

With an exploding burst of sound, shouts and screams, the sentries break out from the stables and brandish their weapons as they run towards the Force, which disintegrates into a greater state of disorder than it resembled just moments before. Men begin running in any of a dozen directions, but in the main towards the west and away from the angry horde behind them. It takes a few seconds before their scared brains and unseeing eyes regain their usual state; then they realise their escape route to the west is blocked by an opposing force of men running towards *them*; this is a small force, but Steve lets loose his dog, which bounds ahead, barking and with bared teeth is soon upon the Force.

A loud *crack* brings an involuntary halt. Gunfire? A second *crack* from the west; it is Bruce with his whip, yet the effect is much as it would have been if the sound *had* been gunfire.

It takes no more than two minutes for the Force to submit to the opposing islanders. Some of the latter continue to show aggression, at times shouting insults and threats and those so inclined advance, waving their weapons.

I come out of the main building and shout for quiet, turn to look at the excited islanders and motion with my arms and hands for them to calm down. I then turn to the petrified Restless ones.

'I'm Ned Youd. None of you are going anywhere unless I say so. Nobody will get hurt, provided you behave yourselves and submit to my directions. Now, who is your leader?' The response is silence, but several pairs of eyes turn towards one man – Nigel.

A stalemate of sorts eventuates. I arrange for some sentries to isolate Nigel and Meg from the Force while Tom and I move out of earshot.

'It looks to me, Ned, that Robert's plan involved the Force being divided into two or three groups and we've subdued one group, perhaps the largest one. Obviously, the plan called for individuals to get into the old city and form up at one or other designated spot. Each group would have its own spot and its own leader.'

'That appears likely, Tom. Today's the day, I guess, when the whole Force is to get into the city; if not today, then tomorrow at the latest. We haven't planned on checking for any night moves, but that's also a possibility. I'm curious, though, as to why Nigel wasn't at the head of his troops all the way.'

'Yeah, what happened here was a mistake, but by whom? Did Robert plan it that way, or did Nigel decide to make his own way to Elwick?'

'Do you recall what John and Mary said at Barrington: that Nigel does what he's told? That would suggest he'd not have initiated his move here separate from his troops; it must have been part of Robert's plan, Tom.'

Tom is quiet for a moment and then he says he has a plan as well.

'What say we talk to Nigel's troops here along these lines: that they were poorly led – in fact, not led at all – but they shouldn't blame Nigel? We can point out that *Robert* was the one who told Nigel to come to Elwick on his own. We *could* have intercepted this group as it approached the Bowen bridge and Nigel, standing here, would not have known a thing about it. Further, it suggests Robert thought Nigel's troops – this group of thirty odd – were dispensable. In short, let's point out to them that Robert's plan contains two serious errors:

> - The individuals that make up his Force are just that. They are not disciplined in any military sense and he was wrong to assume they could put up any resistance if they were to meet an opposing force.

- While that was a serious error, he also assumed all would be resolved in his favour once each group of men had come under direct control of the group's designated leader. Nigel is Robert's son, but Robert erred in choosing him to lead this group. Any decent leader would not have stood idle while knowing his group was leaderless and at risk.'

'I like that, Tom. It puts Robert's ability to judge people under the spotlight.'

'Yes, his whole plan depends on him selecting great leaders and we think he fails that test. Nepotism is a disastrous way to run a rebellion. John and Mary were puzzled at what the attraction was between Robert and Wayne, remember? Whatever Robert did see in Wayne, John's remark implies *he* did not see Wayne as a leader. With luck, we should be able to turn these amateur troops at Elwick back into individuals and have them decide to return to their homes and immerse themselves in the islanders' culture instead of following the Restless culture.'

I'm satisfied with Tom's plan. For all his talk, he *does* think! I continue, 'Let's discuss what we can do to counter Robert's other group or groups. I suggest we send Harry and his horse to Government House to explain what transpired and to ask if anyone there could help monitor the third bridge for twenty four hours starting tonight. We're close enough to Bridgewater to tell the sentries from there to return and take up an intense watch tonight and all day tomorrow.'

'Okay Ned, however before they go from here we should get all sentries to pool whatever knowledge they have about Nigel's troops. Names, addresses, etc.. *Real* names, I mean, not the names they use within Robert's Force.'

'Can you start on this task right away, Tom? We have to make sure that Robert or some other dictator-type doesn't try to start a new rebellion in a year or two's time. I'm getting tired of hunting Restless ones and I'm old enough to claim a pension, though I know there's none who'll grant me one.'

'Yes, me too. Your daughters are too nice for this task.'

'So, I'm not nice, then?'

'That's right.'

'Grrr! But *you've* got a son, Tom.'

'He keeps out of my way, the lazy sod!'

'One final thing; I'll set up sentries to guard the approaches to the racecourse, just in case Robert or one of his groups decides to pay us a visit tonight.'

Cont'd →

13-   <u>**Fight at Bridgewater**</u>

I'll need to hand the reins to Kinjo again,
so he can explain what happened later that
night at Bridgewater.

It was dark when Tim and I arrived back at the southern causeway sentry post and found a chaotic scene. Four sentries were
on the ground being attended to by others while the remaining
sentries were in an agitated state.

Something had happened, but it took Tim and me a fair
while to piece together *what* had transpired. It seemed seven
Restless ones had brushed aside the sentries on the bridge, had
run along the causeway and did not slow down at the southern
end despite encountering the larger group of sentries there. The
invaders carried wooden stakes and used these to fight off their
opponents before heading south and disappearing. It was already
dark and the sentries soon lost sight of them.

I realised that we would have been walking in the opposite direction to these Restless ones, but for some reason we
missed each other.

'We - mm - took an easier path, Kinjo, compared to the -
mm - usual path taken by persons going south on their way - mm
- to the city centre. That's the - mm - shorter route, but it's quite
hilly. From Elwick, we could - mm - have taken to the hills as
well. I - mm - thought about it, but we had no reason to; I reckon
we'd - mm - had enough exercise for one day.'

'Well, we're lucky we did choose your path.'

'Yeah, but the two - mm - paths come close to each other
near Elwick, so - mm - right now, those thugs might be wreaking
havoc at the racecourse.'

We walked across the river to our old sentry post and Tim
explained the situation to the sentries, 'We're asked to maintain

a watch - mm - on the bridge through the next 24 hours so let's - mm - set up shifts to cover this.'

The sentries settled down in the uncertain quiet. Those on duty during the night found it hard to stay alert. Mostly, they walked back and forth in front of the bridge; if they ever stopped, it was not long before they yawned and their eyelids drooped. The stress of the day's happenings contributed to their need for sleep. Walking also helped the time to pass until the sun came up.

It was now June 10. Nobody had attempted to cross the bridge in the dark. I soon had a fish on my line. I stoked the fire back into life and the aroma of grilled fish prompted a few others to try their luck.

14-   **The Real Battlefront**

A cold morning greets us at Elwick. The night has passed without incident, surprising in a way as Nigel's troops could have attempted to break out of their confinement at the racecourse. Their passive state suggests that they *have* nowhere to go; their role in the Force is to be centred on Elwick. I call everyone to attention:

'I see no point in all of us staying here much longer. I will form a small committee to interview anyone wishing to abandon the Force. If successful, you will be escorted back over the Bowen and released.'

I ask Tom to pick two men to help him conduct the interviewing; their task to record the names and addresses of those who seek to return home. There isn't a stampede, but by mid-morning around eighteen men have departed. A head count reveals another eighteen remain in addition to Nigel and Meg. Tom reckons that yesterday's talk, when I pointed to Robert's errors in planning, has sunk in.

Yesterday, everything pointed to today being when Robert's Force will be in the old capital and seeking to occupy the key objectives that he had selected. Yet, where is he? Where is the other half of his Force? Which objectives are his targets? I have to give Robert credit for keeping these specific details controlled. If Nigel knew the details, he isn't saying, but it is pretty clear that Nigel's troops were no more informed than Tom and me.

We can't just sit tight at Elwick. We *have* to go somewhere to the south, I guess, but *where*?

Helen arrives, her horse in lather.

'Robert's here', she says before dismounting. I draw her aside so Nigel and the others can't hear.

'Where's "here" precisely?'

'He came over the southern bridge at dawn. He had ten to fifteen men with him and they were armed with wooden stakes and iron bars. Mr Weeding recognised Dick Loone, your Robert, as he crossed the bridge. The sentries couldn't stop them and they headed around the Domain Hill towards the old city centre. I rode up to Government House to warn those there. I didn't wait for more, but came straight here. Jean had left before me this morning to check on the situation at Bridgewater and she couldn't be long away from here now.'

I tell her to rest a while and give her horse a spell until Jean arrives. Tom and I debate what to do. 'I hope the volunteers we asked for did eventuate and have stationed themselves at Parliament House.'

Tom seems not to notice what I've said. Instead, he draws a breath and presents me with a *new* plan.

'I reckon Nigel's role is to supervise the occupation force. I mean, he is to stay at Elwick until he gets word that Robert's men have gained control of some building or object. Nigel and his men will then leave here and "populate" that place, so to speak. You know, Nigel might not even *know* where Robert's targets are. It could be that Government House is where Nigel's gang is to head; that would be a quite sensible place to settle in, assuming Robert's targets are near the city centre. Meg's presence here lends support to this possibility. You know, give a woman the task of putting the house in order. Mind you, I have a feeling that Meg is here to put some backbone in Nigel.'

'Yeah, that all makes sense and it proves we are wasting our time here. He's a clever bugger is Robert; fancy not trusting his son well enough to let him in on the details!'

'Clever maybe, but ruthless and, I surmise, confident in his ability to carry his whole Force on his shoulders. Maybe the other leaders, as we've presumed must exist, are no more aware of his grand plan than we are.'

'So, Tom, a leader might only know what *his* role is?'

'Could be; having lived his life in our island environment, where he has had to keep hidden his keenness to revive the Restless culture, suggests secrecy would have to be second nature to Robert.'

'Well, Tom, what now?'

'I'd like to hear what Jean has to tell us about Bridgewater, but rather than have us all waiting, I suggest we split our forces in two and you lead your half south as fast as you can. Harry and his horse have just arrived, so I will keep him. I'll wait until Jean arrives, then I'll send Harry to catch up to you and give you the news and he can then be your forward scout searching for evidence of Robert's whereabouts. I'll follow with my half of our men. We'll leave Nigel and his troops here. If I'm right, he won't dare leave here before he gets word from Robert.'

'You *have* been thinking, Tom!'

I set off south with twenty men, all spoiling for a fight after they heard how Robert's men had broken past the southern sentries by force. Bruce knows the streets and he leads us onto what was once the railway line linking the city centre with Bridgewater; this line had been torn up some years prior to the collapse of the Restless culture and replaced by a cycle way. The beauty of going this way is that it minimises the need to climb hills, though it is quite overgrown with shrubs and weeds now and it does need some effort to walk through this growth. I tell the men about the "mystery" bloke who had evaded a Bridgewater sentry somewhere near Pottery Creek Road and they tell me we are near this road. I choose to stop while I begin instructing a few of the men to check out the old hydroelectricity power control centre, but Harry arrives with the news of last night's clash at Bridgewater and my men are now even *angrier*.

I venture to conclude that the Force has been split into three groups, two of which are Robert's elite, commando regiments intent on gaining control of a small number of targets, while the third group – Nigel's mob – are held in reserve. This would make it easier for Robert to ensure secrecy will prevail. It also implies that if I can marshal my troops at just one or two places, we will have the larger force. My challenge is to decide *where* to head. Harry can soon round up all the volunteers. The sentries at the bridges are no longer needed there; instead, they should be instructed to head towards the city centre and link up with my men or with Tom's men. Harry heads off on this errand, going first to Government House and then the southern bridge before riding to Bridgewater.

It makes sense now to wait for Tom's group to catch up, before I send anyone along Pottery Creek Road. A few of us move to the nearby Main Road, just in case Tom has elected to take the road instead of the cycle way. He arrives not long after and he has both horsewomen with him.

'How can I thank you, Tom – you're a genius.'

'Just plant five hectare of spuds on my farm when this is all over, Ned.'

Tom asks Jean to ride to the vicinity of the hydro control centre to see if there are any people loitering about or any signs of recent activity. The place is apparently just over a kilometre away; anyway she is soon back.

'I saw one man who I think heard the sound of my horse's hooves and went behind a building. No other signs of activity, but people could have been inside.'

There are now forty of us. Tom says, 'let's send ten men, including Steve and his dog, to search that place, accompanied by Jean to provide liaison with us, while we head south with Helen going ahead on her horse to locate Restless ones.'

We do as Tom suggests. After a while, we have left most of the houses behind us and are walking beside what once were shops and office buildings; on occasions the sounds of our footsteps echo between their glass frontages.

Helen returns – with *real* news!

'There's a right royal ding dong in front of Parliament House.'

She says we are about 800 metres away and we quicken our step. Soon we hear angry cries and shouts ahead of us and, breasting the hill that lies between us and the melee, we look down on the struggle. I find it hard to decide who is fighting who and who is winning. We run down the slope, shouting as loud as we can and Bruce flexes his arm too – a frightening sound that whip makes when you're not expecting it.

The battle scene changes immediately. Men break away from whoever they've been fighting and head along the water-front, chased by other men. The fighting stops.

'Hi, I'm Ned Youd. Is anyone in charge here?'

It is then that I see two men being restrained by other men.

'G'day, Ned, 'tis good you've come. We're about pooped, I'm afraid, but we stopped them buggers from gettin' inside!'

I shake his hand. He says he's from Premadena and he and his mates have spent two days "cooling their heels" as he puts it, but today has made up for the wait.

'We've grabbed two blokes for you. Don't know any-thing about 'em except that they were too bloody slow to get away.'

Tom and I walk across to this small group. As usual, Tom does the talking. 'Where are you two thugs from and what's your names?'

'Get stuffed!'

'That won't do. You're not going anywhere until you explain why you're here. Robert can't free you. We've already decimated his reserve force. Nigel is still wondering what hit him and soon our main regiment and its crack fighters will be here to give you a hard time, just for the fun of it. Matter of fact, I'm going to enjoy watching what happens.'

I try not to laugh while Tom continues to lay it on real

thick.

Pointing to one man, Tom says, 'Come on, what's your name?'

'William.'

'That's not what I mean. Your *real* name is the name we recognise on this island.'

I move forward, punch the bloke hard on the jaw; he crumples and I turn to the other man.

'Well?'

'Ned's a softy when he talks,' Tom says. Smiling, he continues, 'He has other means to get what he wants. What's your name?'

Two tongues loosen and at last we start to learn some useful information. Their task was to capture Parliament House; they were six and they'd been led to believe it would be empty or almost empty.

'What's Robert's real name?'

Silence! I move forward again.

'We don't know, honestly we don't', they chorus.

'Who is your leader?'

'Reginald.'

I move forward yet again, but the chap from Premadena intervenes, 'The Reginald bloke introduced himself at the start. He ran away when you came over the hill. If my blokes catch him, I'll point him out to you.'

Tom says, 'Fair enough, where's Robert?'

'He's not here.'

I find myself standing eye to eye with the two Restless ones. It takes but an instant to bang their heads together, with the desired effect.

'He went away somewhere with about eight men before we reached here. We came over the bridge together, but that was a coincidence. It wasn't supposed to be that way. I think we were supposed to cross an hour after him, but he was delayed.'

'*Hmm!*', Tom says, 'maybe his clock stopped, or perhaps he thought there was safety in the extra numbers you blokes could give him. Which explanation is the correct one, do you think?'

I have to admire Tom; he's quick-witted for a farmer.

At this point, the front door of Parliament House opens and two men step outside. One is grey-haired, the other much younger.

'I'm Mick Bourke and this is my grandson. We want to thank all you fine men for fight'n those bastards.'

The younger man kicks the shins of the captives, who collapse in pain. Tom looks down at them and says, '*Get up! I haven't finished with you yet. Explain to me why you chose to commit yourselves to support Robert's plan when you don't know his real name and it seems to me that you don't know what that plan is?'

The two men look at each other. Are they wondering who will break first, or is each man struggling to invent a reason that could sound plausible while not being the real reason? Tom says, 'I can wait, but your stories had better be good ones.'

There's a commotion behind me. Some sentries from the bridge, who would have been on the receiving end of this morning's brutal crossing by Robert and his merry men, have caught a Restless one and it is clear this bloke is going to have two black eyes for a while.

'Reginald', says the man from Premadena softly.

Tom moves across to have a chat.

'Some leader you are, scaredy-pants. Fancy deserting your troops just because you figured you were quick enough to save your own skin. Pity you didn't run away from that recent meeting at Camp 18. Your wife would still recognise you if you had, though I doubt she will after Ned has his way with you. I can help you escape his wrath, if you're honest. For instance, what's your real name and where do you live when you're not doing Dick Loone's dirty business for him?'

'No comment.'

Tom steps aside, saying; 'Over to you, Ned. This idiot *is* an idiot.'

I wasn't born to generations of world wood chopping champions for nothing. I bring my hands down hard past each side of Reginald's head – just inside of his shoulder joints. If I'd been standing on a log with my axe in my hands, I'd have been very pleased with the result. My action has the desired effect now, though, so I am still quite pleased. Reginald, fearsome leader, is now in pain and shock on the ground. *Stunned.* Good, I think – I doubt I'll need to do that again.

Tom then returns to the first two captives.

'Robert plays for keeps and so do we when our culture is threatened. Now, you two, answer the question you've been thinking about while I was so rudely interrupted by your bloody snot-faced leader. Look at him – still on the ground. At least, you're standing. That's a good sign, isn't it? I wouldn't want Ned to do his next trick, so speak up.'

I have to think what this trick of mine will be. A quick kick in the balls perhaps, or a broken arm would also do and it would be a more lasting reminder. Yes, that would do.

15-　　**<u>A Bargain Struck</u>**

One of the captives begins to speak.

'My grandparents lived with us when I was growing up. They told us what life was like before the chaotic end to the world. They hoped their lifestyle would continue, but it didn't. They had to leave the city or they'd have starved and they damn near starved anyway, because they weren't the first to leave and the thousands who went before them gobbled up all the food within four days walk of the Derwent.'

'They were stupid', Tom says.

'They were not stupid.'

'Yes they were. It should have been as plain as the noses on their faces even *thirty years* before the collapse that Western Civilisation *would* collapse and that the city was unsustainable – all cities were and had been for centuries. If they'd been smart, they'd have moved to the countryside at that time and started to live sustainably.'

'That's hindsight talking. The city was their life. They were educated, with good jobs and a good house. They wanted for nothing. When they did find a place in the country to start again, they had nothing; the house was a "hovel" they said and the shops were poor. There was nothing worth buying and con-versations were tiresome – all about the weather and who won the latest game of whichever sport was being played at the time. The latest fashions, the hottest new play or movie, the upcoming lecture at the university; these were topics that my grandpar-ents missed. And the politics, of course; the power shift from the Lower House, the abolishment of political parties and emer-gence of people-power instead, all took place in the early years after they left the city. They were left out; as "city people", the islanders wanted nothing to do with them and of course they knew nobody. They longed for the city life they'd known and it was their dream to be able to return to the city.'

'So, here you are a hundred years later with five mates and you're going to dust off all the dust and restart Parliament! Now, that's the wackiest dream anyone's told me since I met Robert two weeks ago. Seems to me, you're no smarter than your stupid grandparents.'

Tom continues his probing. He is enjoying the task.

'What kind of pie-in-the-sky tale did Robert tell you to get you to come here?'

The other captive makes to answer, but Tom cuts him short, 'I'll get to you next. Your mate is going to give me his answer.'

'Robert came to see us, my wife and myself, just over ten years ago. He invited us to join a group of people who longed to see a return of the Western Civilisation to the island. He was short on details, except that he wanted us to choose new first names to use in the meetings he said were regular features of his plan. Upper class names were best, he said, and not nicknames. I chose William. Robert said that was not a distinguished name; I argued that it was good enough for English kings and I did not know of a King Robert.

'My wife wasn't much interested. Her ancestors had long been on the land and we often argued about how precious city life must have been. Of course, neither of us had personal experience to go on, but I would recall what my grandparents told me.'

'Does your wife know why you came here?'

'She thinks I've gone fishing up the Lakes.'

'Boy, are you going to be in trouble when you get home – assuming you're capable of that after Ned's had his fun.'

Tom is about to start on the other captive when a group comes over the hill and down to where we are standing. It's the men we'd sent along Pottery Creek Road and they are in good spirits.

'We've saved the island for you, Ned. There were five Restless ones there, but we soon stitched them up well and good. You should have seen Brutus go!'

Brutus wags his tail. I ask where they are now.

'We tied each one to wire fences. There are plenty of those around the electrical equipment. And plenty of electrical cable too, so we used that. Each bloke is at least 20 metres away from the others. We figured they could stay like that until you've had a chance to question them.'

'Did you find out their leader's name?'

'He said his name was Charles.'

'What did they plan to do?'

'They had sheets and sheets of electricity networks spread on the floor. Large drawings they were and it seemed a couple of the blokes knew how to read them.'

'Where's Jean and Helen?'

'They're trotting around the city centre.'

'Well done fellows, and Brutus.' The dog comes over and waits for me to pat its head.

Nigel's mob initially numbered 32, 33 with Nigel, and Reginald's consisted of six. Charles' mob was five and it was said Robert had eight of his own when he crossed the bridge. Total 52. I felt sure Wayne would be one leader, so if there were sixty at the Camp 18 meeting, Wayne could have seven in his group. *Seven*: There were seven thugs in the group that forced its way across at Bridgewater.

I take Tom aside.

'There's much to be learned here and at Pottery Creek Road, but the two *key* groups are still on the loose. Robert has one and Wayne, I suspect, has the other. I'm worried that Government House is under attack, or soon will be. We've got to find Robert and Wayne. I want to split our group in two; there are almost fifty of us now. Send one half to guard Government House, taking Steve and Brutus with them, and the other half can stay here until we learn where Robert or Wayne are.'

'Do you and I take one half each?'

'Yes. You can continue the questioning. They've been softened up sufficiently, I reckon and you can always remind them of my interviewing style. I wish we had closer links with Jean and Helen. If one turns up here, suggest that they each report to you often. Even "no report" is of value because it gives you the chance to provide them with new instructions. Tell them where my group is too. If I find Government House is quiet, I'll leave my men there and I'll come back here and we can go to Pottery Creek Road and have some more fun.'

I select my group and we set off. I make sure all the men from Government House who joined us two days ago are with me, except Bruce, who I feel could be useful to have in Tom's group; that whip speaks the same language I do.

My group strides out from Parliament House at great speed, so much so that I am content to bring up the rear. We climb the hill and all seems normal until we come level with Government House and see evidence of a fight. We break into a run, round the corner and see the front door. A body lies to one side. 'It's John', someone says. The rest of us burst through the open doorway and are met by several women, some shrieking, and by clutches of petrified children.

'Where are they, the men?' I shout.

'We chased them towards the pub not long ago. Hurry, you'll probably catch them.'

'Any of you injured?'

'Most of us are hurting, but none are serious – I think.'

'John's come to', says a man behind me, 'He's got a bad gash on his skull. We'll have to check how serious it is.'

'Okay, let's go after them.'

Brutus bursts ahead of us and soon begins barking. The sound leads us to the left of the pub, along a path to a part of the farm. In the distance we see groups of men fighting – until Brutus reaches them. The fighting stops and some men turn to run north, away from us, though not fast enough, because Brutus is up to the task. It is a joy to watch him round up any man who tries to sneak away.

We reach the mob and our numbers do the trick. Each thug is held by two, if not three, men. Brutus runs around and around the whole group; nobody is going to escape the retribution being handed out by my men. I see George Weeding, but not his father. As if he knows my thoughts, George says, 'Dad's out to it in the pub. He got hit on the head by the bloke I think is their leader' and he points to a man on the opposite side of the melee. I look – Wayne!

My men are giving all the thugs a real working-over. I walk to where Wayne is standing or, I realise, is being propped up by two men while two more are punching and kicking him as hard as they can.

'Let him be for a moment, fellows. You can have him back after I've finished with him.'

Wayne turns towards the sound of my voice. Both his eyes are closed, black and blue and swollen.

'A couple of weeks ago, you laughed when Robert and you walked away and left me chained to that bloody tree. I'm tempted to laugh at you now, but instead WHERE IS ROBERT?' The words are shouted in Wayne's left ear.

'Fat hope! I don't know because he never told me.'

'Just stand still while I prepare to break your arm.'

I grab his right arm below the elbow and twist it sharply backwards. He winces in pain.

'Just testing, Wayne; I'll have another go.'

'Wait! I'll tell you what I know, but I do *not* know Robert's plan.'

'Well, now we're talking, just keep in mind that I have hold of your arm. Any bullshit from you and your arm *will* break.

Let's start with you telling me whose idea it was for your group here to consist of ruthless thugs who delight in bashing innocent people over the head with stakes and iron bars?'

Wayne hesitates.

'I don't have time to wait while you invent some story. I have to find Robert. His group is the last of the initial five sections of the Force still at large. The other 50 something men have been captured and none of them are going to achieve their parts of Robert's grand plan.' I jerk his arm back.

'Both. I said I wanted, you know, to choose and Robert said that was fine, but he had plans for, you know, allocating many of the men to other groups, so he gave me around twenty names, you know, and said I could select seven from those men.'

'Most members of the Force are not so tough, so it seems you two are an evil duo; ruthless! I know what Robert *says* his intentions are, but just as his real name is not Robert, I believe his real reasons are different. What was your reason for joining his Force?'

'If you knew my real name, you know, you could understand. My grandfather was in prison for a while. My father suffered, you know, from this, 'cos the island society saw our family as up to no good. Dad could not get a decent job and, you know, our farm was small and barely enough to live on. I was, you know, shunned at school. You know, Robert seemed to offer a chance to re-balance that situation; if he, you know, could bring back the Restless culture, I would have a chance to point out, you know, that my grandfather did his time; he was released, he didn't, you know, escape and he didn't commit a new crime. After the collapse, you know, that record was ignored; once a crook, you know, always a crook. Even me, his grandson, am lumbered with that charge.'

I begin to develop a plan for how to turn Wayne into a supporter; with luck, his men might change allegiance too. They are all Restless ones with a backbone, prepared to fight.

'I knew I would, you know, be expected to play rough here in the old city, but that's, you know, what everybody *expects* me to do, so I joined the Force.'

'What was your group's task today?'

'To takeover Government House; Robert told me it would, you know, be occupied, to expect a fight, but I found, you know, the people living there were ready. We didn't catch them by surprise and I sensed, you know, they outnumbered us. It wasn't easy to control the fight. A few, you know, of the women were demons too.'

'If you'd succeeded here, were you to tackle another task?'

'Not today. Robert, you know, was going to check the status of all his groups, you know, and he might have wanted us to help someplace else if things had not gone to plan.'

'Tom reckoned Nigel's group was supposed to occupy the House once the Force had pacified it. Correct?'

'Maybe. I don't know what Nigel is doing.'

'He's staying well out of the fighting.'

'Pity – I could have used his men.'

'I'm not sure they'd have helped. His group was as far away from being a fighting force as you could get and half of them deserted when we caught them.'

'*Bloody Hell!*'

I laugh. Things *are* swinging my way!

'I'm intrigued how you were able to keep your name; Wayne is not upper class.'

'Maybe not, but I said I wanted, you know, to have that name and Robert didn't argue.'

Two weeks ago, in fact even just yesterday, had I encountered Wayne in his present state, I'd have knocked his block off, but I found I was sympathising with him. He struck me as a decent man who'd been dealt a poor deal in life. More to the point, he was emerging as a real ally if I played my cards right.

I'm sure Tom would have been quick to put a proposition to him, but in his absence, I decide to do my best and strike now.

'I'm becoming convinced that Robert needed you. You were an integral part of his plan from the beginning. He needed enforcers and I think he chose you based on that reputation of yours. I am *sure* you do not need Robert. His plan is in shreds. With eight men, he can't capture and hold any place of sufficient importance that the islanders would stop and take notice. I am going to offer you a bargain. Get your group together now and explain to them that they are no longer to consider themselves part of Robert's Force. As soon as my men have noted their real names, they will be free to return to their homes or, if they prefer, they can join my men and help us find and defeat Robert's group.

'I am going to keep you close to me and you will help me find Robert. Play your new role straight and I won't break your arm. When this event is all over, I will talk with Elders in your Clan and in any other territory you suggest, and I will urge them to take note of the unfairness of your reputation. Also, I will not seek to have a black mark placed against your name as a consequence of your role in the Force.'

'What if I say no to your offer?'

I twist his arm again.

'All bets will be off. Your arm will be broken and you will be accused by me of being a key leader of the Force, second only to Robert in importance, which I think would be a fair accusation. Then, you *will* have a reputation in the community!'

16-   __The Trap__

While I wait, Wayne plays his part and two of his mates join my group. We do our best to patch up the injured at Government House, though I have a struggle to explain why three attackers are now my friends. It looks as if no serious injuries have resulted. I leave ten of my men at the House and take the remainder, including Brutus and Steve and my new-found "friends" to where I'd left Tom.

I can't get one question out of my head. How on earth did Robert manage to entrance his followers with hints of his dream, the re-emergence on the island of the Restless culture, while keeping the details of his plan so well controlled within his own head? Also, I want to know how he could conduct himself as Dick Loone; how he could live in his Clan territory without people sensing that he had a second life – as Robert, the ultimate Restless one. He had a son, but did he still have a wife?

Tom shows surprise when he sees me arm-in-arm with Wayne, until I reveal the type of grip I have on his arm and point out his limited ability to see anything.

'You will note', I say, 'my negotiation skills can be quite effective, don't you agree?'

Helen had come by with no news, other than that she had contacted Jean and asked her to visit Government House.

It is strange that Robert has gone to ground. His target for today has to be somewhere in or near the old city centre, the one-time home of political power over the island.

I prompt Wayne to recollect any conversations he'd had with Robert about the city, about places and about how to strike a blow that would startle the islanders. 'These things must have been on Robert's mind ten years ago, or whenever it was that he first contacted you. Did the two of you become drinking buddies, did tongues ever loosen?'

'Robert didn't drink. He was strait-laced, you know, and he was never the life of the party. He was, you know, always in control. In part, I think, you know, that was an aspect that appealed. You know, he had a mission and he gave the impression of being able to achieve it.'

'As if he was a modern-day Jesus and his followers had to be *believers*.'

'I guess you could say that. You know, he wasn't a warm person, but I put *my* faith in his being able to achieve what he said was his goal. His followers, you know, had many reasons for attending his camp meetings. Perhaps, most of them could be thought to be loners, you know – for whatever reason, they did not fit in to whichever territory they lived in, you know; at Robert's meetings, they found company, friends to talk with.'

'Well, I want to find Robert *now*.'

Tom and I discuss what to do. Wayne listens in, as I have not reached the stage of trusting him and I keep a grip on his arm.

'There are more than fifty of us now, Ned. A few more sentries arrived from their bridge duty while you were away. There are also Mick Bourke's three sons we can count on. They were all away fishing when the fight started this morning. We could set a couple of our men to keep Reginald quiet; I don't think he has quite recovered yet from meeting you. The two I've been grilling won't cause any harm now.'

'Are you proposing we divide into several groups and fan out in search of Robert?'

'We could, though I accept that we could end up wasting everybody's time and the value of our numerical size could be lost.'

'Yeah, that worries me. Will it be long before the horse-women return?'

'I expect one at least to be quite close. Let's wait until we can discuss plans with whoever turns up first. They are our eyes, really, just as you are Wayne's eyes, Ned.'

'Are you suggesting you want to hold Helen's hand?'

'Hell no! You know me.'

'That's why I asked.'

While we wait, I tell Wayne of the skirmish at Pottery Creek Road and ask if he knows Charles.

'Yes, though not too, you know, closely. I believe his ancestors were bigwigs, you know, in the old city, wealthy, and I gather he dreamed of being like them, you know. I think he worked for a blacksmith, so quite a come-down, eh?'

'I'm not upset by all the tales I've heard over the past few hours, of descendants of prosperous city people being "forced" to live impoverished lives since the collapse. You are the one exception, Wayne. I reckon you do have a legitimate complaint. Before the collapse, the islanders who lived outside the city were ignored by those *same* city people who had it so good. *They* milked the farmers and others in country towns who worked like slaves to keep the city-dwellers fed and who also contributed more than a fair share of tax each year too, once you take into account that most of that tax money never went to help country dwellers – it went to help Charles' ancestors and others like them.'

Tom had been listening. 'Well said, Ned. I went close to kicking that bloke who denied his grandparents were stupid. He hadn't understood how blind they were to who was *allowing* them to live the high life. University lectures, fiddlesticks! None of my ancestors had ever *seen* the university and the university never saw them – it was *expected* that they had to go to the city if they wanted the education and they were too busy to leave their farm.'

Helen turns up. 'John is Jean's husband, so Jean needs to look after him.'

I decide it is time to set a plan. 'Helen, you and Jean have spent half the day riding around the city centre and no sign has yet turned up of Robert's group. Can you think how the whole lot of us might have better luck?'

'The city streets are real quiet, sound-wise I mean, so Robert could know where I was by the clip clop of my horse. *Maybe* he has had time to hide whenever Jean or I came close.'

'So, we might have more chance if our men jogged around the streets in twos or threes.'

'Yes, Tom, that's worth a try', I say. 'Let's plan the routes, though, and give each group an hour, say, to cover their area. The sun's not shining so they'll have to estimate the time.'

'Make it four to a group, with two of them asked to scan the floors above ground with their eyes as they go, working one side of the street each. The other two can test entrance doors they go past to look for any sign of recent use. There's a lot of dust around, Ned. The streets haven't been swept for a century, of course. It's a pity we don't have several more like Brutus; he smells his quarry.'

'Right, we'll send out eight teams of four. Helen, you live here, so you can draw the best map of the search zone. Most of us are country yokels.'

It takes a while to set this up, then it is back to waiting.

'Tom, do you ever stand around waiting for your carrots to grow? I'm always on the go on my farm.'

'Of course, I spend weeks at a time just watching the little blighters.'

Wayne interrupts our earnest conversation.

'The State Library might be worth a visit. Robert often brought a book to meetings, you know. You hardly ever see *anyone* holding a book, so it intrigued me. Once, when he wasn't looking, you know, I opened his book and saw stamped in it "Property of State Library." You know, I doubt the Library would be a key target in his plan, but it could be of personal interest, you know, if he had some free time.'

I turn to Steve; 'If you know where the Library is, can you and Brutus go and search the building? It can't do any harm to try.'

It is getting dark and this search will need to be our last effort today. I don't believe we could find anyone in the dark unless they were careless or stupid and Robert is neither.

Waiting is not something I'm used to. I turned my attention to Reginald who was now standing and still being guarded by two of our men.

'Tom, did you get much useful information from Reginald?'

'The bare minimum, I'd say. Maybe he knows no more, but you could show us all your new-found negotiation skills, if you'd like.'

'Remember me, Reginald? I'd like to understand how someone as intelligent as Robert could believe that you'd make a good leader, in fact in the top four chosen for this plan of his.'

'I put my hand up.'

I shake my head in disbelief. 'You mean, Robert asked for volunteers and you were the one who responded?'

'Not quite, but I think Robert's plan recognised the fact that we who attended his meetings were not the makings of an army. That's why I and the others, including Wayne here, were given one limited task each. Perhaps he was prepared for a failure to achieve one of his objectives. I'm sure that Parliament House would not have been his highest priority target.'

'*Hmmm*, you're hoping that's the case aren't you! I'd have thought he'd have been better off to boost the numbers in Wayne's group. Wayne was given a key target to capture and he found it was well defended.

'Anyway, what led you to join Robert's gang of whining misfits? Is he a Messiah?'

'Nigel works for me.'

'That's hilarious. Neither of you could organize a chook

raffle, yet you both became group leaders in the Force. Robert had to be plain dumb crazy to have persisted with his plan knowing how weak the Force was. In real life, what do you and Nigel do?'

'We're fencing contractors in Trayapana territory.'

'Do your fences say up for long?'

'Too right, they do!'

'Well, I do my own fencing. Was it Nigel who talked you into attending Robert's meetings?'

'No. Robert talked me into employing Nigel and he explained his intention was to sometime succeed in re-introducing the Restless culture here. That interested me.'

Wayne is still with me as I chat with Reginald.

'Let's go back to the meeting at Camp 18. Each of you, I gather, was given your target by Robert and a number of men were assigned to you. What were your instructions assuming you succeeded in securing those targets?'

'I reckon you know more than I did, Ned. I was told, you know, to maintain control at Government House until someone would arrive to confirm our success. I assumed, you know, we would be asked to do something else and I guessed my group would be relieved, you know, by others so we could do that. It was you who said Nigel had the relief force, wasn't it?'

'We're supposing it was Nigel, because his large group might have been capable of occupying an area. They could not have captured anything!'

'Robert told me to control Parliament House until he came by with more men.'

'I wonder what Charles' instructions were. Speak of which, I wonder how they'll pass the night up close to their fences. I'm in no mood to waste time on them now.'

Speaking up, Wayne says, 'Isn't there a risk Robert's group, you know, could free them before tomorrow?'

'Fair question! Tom and I had assumed we'd have located Robert by now, so there was little chance of the Pottery Creek mob being helped before we got there to deal with them.

'Do you know where Robert lived, Wayne – the Clan?'

'Not exactly, though based on the regular meetings, it occurred to me, you know, that he may have been from around Longford, as that, you know, would cause him least trouble getting to and from meetings.'

'Were there many locations?'

'Six, though a couple were only used once, you know. Most meetings were at 16, 18 and 20. Camp 21 was for special occasions – men only, you know, as I'm sure you noticed.'

'Where were they all?'

'18 you know. 16 …'

'We knew 18 existed. We don't know where it was.'

'Oh, well 18 is near Meander, 16 is close to Nile and 20 is not far from Blessington.'

'Hey, Tom – did you hear that? Camp 18 is in *our* territory, maybe within fifteen km of your farm. Well, I'll be blowed, how cheeky of Robert!'

Tom pulls a long face, as if he's wondering how he could have missed detecting that camp. Wayne continues.

'I wouldn't, you know, put too much faith in my idea of Longford. I guess you'd be better off trying to find the Loones.'

'Yes. We've now collected a lot of names, well over thirty *real* ones, not the ones Robert uses. I can't wait to hand them to Clan Elders. In most cases, the individuals can just sink back into their communities without recrimination – but not in all cases. I'm disappointed that our request for a police presence in the old city seems not to have been heard. The police would be handy to trace the lives of those on our name list.'

I turn to continue probing Reginald, but Brutus' bark stops me.

'Quiet, Brutus,' says Steve, 'Someone has been in the Library recently, but there was no one in the building when we went in. Brutus has a good nose memory, so if by chance we bump into whoever it was, he'll bark his head off.'

For the second time today, I pat the dog's head. We could do with another half dozen dogs.

The search parties start to return; their news is dismal – no sign of *any* living souls. Seven reports are like that, but where is the eighth group? We wait. It is almost dark now.

Horses hooves! Helen appears from over the hill.

'One team is in a fight. Don't know who with, but they're outnumbered. Can you follow me? They're in Patrick Street.'

'Tom: take all but four of us and *go*.'

With shouts and yells, they disappear behind Helen's horse and head over the hill, with Brutus, bless his soul, in his customary place in front and barking.

17-   <u>A Night Time Ramble</u>

'This gets more puzzling, Wayne. That part of the city has nothing of note, has it?'

'I don't know it, Ned. Do you, Reginald?'

'Me neither.'

Mr Bourke opens his door.

'You can all stay with us tonight, but at least come in and have someth'n to eat. My sons caught a goodly number of fish and we've fresh taters too.'

I ask one man to stay outside in case anyone comes by with news.

'No, bring him in with you. Me youngest son Pat will gladly do that, won't you me boy. We're mighty grateful for what you've done for us today.'

For a while our minds are transported away from the day's conflict. The Bourke's are generous hosts. Home brewed beer is poured for us, the talking gets louder and the six Restless ones begin to relax and join in the many discussions going on in what I was told was once the Lower House chamber.

Mrs Bourke senior and the younger women begin to bring plates with food.

I ask Mr Bourke how he'd come to live here.

'Me father was the youngest of four brothers and their farm in Trayapana territory was not big enough for him to get a useful portion, so he left home. Me Dad guessed there'd be some place in the old city with open land enough for his family after the collapse. He stopped searching when he arrived here. We've three paddocks, twelve acres in all, and we barter with the folks up on the Domain. I was born here.'

There's no word back from Patrick Street. I sense we'll have to pay a visit to Pottery Creek Road tonight. I tell Mr

Bourke, 'I want to take my four men with me to check the situation there. I could tie our six captives to posts before I go, if you've some rope or chains.'

'No need, Ned. I'll make sure they're all drunk soon and my sons can block their access outside. We've plenty of empty rooms upstairs, so they can all be in one room and a son can keep watch at the door of the room. You go now and God speed!'

A man in my group had been present when Charles' mob was captured and his guidance proves useful. There's heavy cloud above; no moonlight reaches us. The meal has helped, I feel, to give us the energy we need to cover the five km in quick time.

The leading man exclaims, 'They're gone! Someone's been here!'

It had to be Robert. *Damn!*

The buildings are dark. We feel our way into the nearest one. No sign of anyone. We move to the other buildings. Same result. I guess that Robert's group of eight would be thirteen and maybe these are now all at Patrick Street.

We head there as best we can; I'm not sure we are taking the shortest route. We find a lot of hills! Helen's sketch showed Patrick Street to be rather long, but I trust we'll find where the fight is by the noise.

Patrick Street: as quiet as a church. I split my group in two and we check out the whole street. Nothing to be seen!

'*Bugger!* Let's head back to the Bourke's. I reckon we can all do with a beer or three now, after this running about in the dark, all for nothing!'

Pat Bourke is still at the front door. 'Nobody's turned up since you left, Ned.'

I don't understand it. By my calculation, Robert's group had to number in the low teens, about thirteen, but Tom would have nigh on three times as many, plus Brutus. How could we lose the fight and, even more puzzling, how could a combined mass of over 50 men simply disappear?

I have to assume that Robert chose discretion over valour and, outnumbered, broke off the combat and headed away in some direction, pursued by Tom. If so, there is no way of finding them before dawn.

Cont'd →

18-   <u>Things Get Serious</u>

Mick Bourke shows me to a room with a *bed*. What luxury!

I can't sleep. After two weeks of sleeping on boards or on the ground, maybe the bed is *too* soft, but I struggle to imagine what could have taken place on Patrick Street and dare not contemplate a situation in which Tom's men had been outnumbered and were now captives of Robert. Had Nigel's mob sprung to life to help Robert, or was Robert in control of a completely separate band of supporters unknown to members of Robert's Force and to us?

If Robert *had* gained control over Tom's men, it changes things. My mind throws up question after question, yet answers are absent. Over and over again, the same questions beg for solutions:

- How *many* men does Robert now control?
- Who *are* these men?
- What is Robert's *real* motive?

A picture begins to form in my mind. Tom and I had puzzled over how Robert could be so bold, or stupid, as to attempt his attack on the old capital with his Force; that small, rag-tag collection of men who quite likely had never even played a proper game of football in their lives. The Force was <u>not</u> an Army!

However, what if Robert had cultivated a separate group of followers; hand-picked for their discipline and aggression? Robert's *real* commandos!

Maybe he planned for the Force to create a sideshow to occupy those who rallied to help me and Tom, so that he could then invade the city with this hidden trump card and catch us off-guard.

His timing begins to look astute. Did he surmise that we'd relieve our bridge sentries of their duty once it appeared the Force was all in the old city, thereby making it simple for his other group to cross the river unseen?

The idea hits me that the reason he sent Nigel to Paradise to "invite" us to Camp 21 was to make sure that we would work to lead a force of islanders to oppose him on a battleground of *his* choosing. That way, if he could eliminate us, he'd ensure that the island's Clans would not be immediately capable of physically opposing him in his endeavours. Tom and I weren't the only islanders who'd sought to catch Restless ones, but everyone considered us the most successful. By comparison, those who might decide to take up the task after us would be rank amateurs and by the time a serious opposition could be mounted, Robert would have consolidated his occupation of the old capital.

In fact, the Members in their Assembly Room might decide to let Robert take over the city; it wasn't a valued part of the island and the city's name brings shudders, not praise.

Phew, what a thought! There's no way I can sleep now! I become impatient waiting for daylight so I can set out to get answers to all these questions.

Will he attack Government House today? And Parliament House? If close to ninety per cent of the men Tom and I had cobbled together are now his prisoners, Robert could quite probably succeed even if his new force was small in numbers.

Dawn at last! I seek out Wayne. At best, I have ten men on "my" side and that number includes Wayne, his two followers, the three Bourke sons plus myself.

'It would appear Tom and his men are now captives of Robert, Wayne. Don't ask me how he managed to do that. I reckon I'm his next target. Tom's become one fly in the spider's web.'

Wayne nods, 'We're vulnerable with, you know, our small numbers in a big city. An ambush would be easy to arrange, you know, and it would succeed unless we had, you know, forward scouts checking places. I've talked, you know, with my two and we'll pitch in to help you. You know, for my part, I can't *believe* the result I dreamed of will now eventuate. You know, my interest in Robert's plan was selfish; my ancestors were never believers of the Restless culture. I wanted, you know, to sweep away the negativity with which islanders view me and my father.'

Encouraging! At least I know now the full strength of my troop – ten.

I decide to send one man to Government House to alert the families to the situation. I am loath to ask them for volunteers to join me; I guess Robert's two goals for today are to capture me and to capture Government House. The families would need everyone at home to form a robust defence.

It seems just a moment before my man returns, with Helen; they'd met each other about 300 metres from where I'm standing.

Disturbing news – Brutus returned home during the night; he'd been in a fight or been bashed and was limping. His left hip was sore – bruised. No sign of Steve.

Helen explains, 'When I saw the fight on Patrick Street, I estimated that the mob attacking our four men numbered around a dozen, but Tom had about 40, so I figured the tables would soon turn in our favour. It was a chaotic scene, or more aptly, it was a clashing of shouts and yells, because it was too dark for me to *see* the action. I could hear Brutus barking.'

'I went there last night, Helen, and checked out the whole street. It was deserted and none of Tom's men have returned here yet. Robert has somehow captured everyone and this must mean he had extra men hidden somewhere other than Patrick Street and Tom was lured to wherever these men were waiting. How's John? Could Jean free herself to help me find Robert?'

'I believe so, but I've no inkling of when she could arrive

here.'

'I suggest you return home straight away, put my request to her and also let the families know that I fear Robert will attack Government House sometime today. I don't know when, because I suspect he has another task planned for today as well – to capture me!

'Please come back here as fast as you can. I will need all the eyes I can muster today. I want to rescue Tom and his men, but not get caught in another ambush myself.'

Helen rides off and it is back to waiting. I relate my thoughts to the Bourke men, who agree to follow my direction despite a risk that Robert could turn his attention to attacking Parliament House as well today.

'I do appreciate your support', I say, 'If I can have Robert focus on me, without getting myself caught by him, it could be that he won't get around to attacking his city targets today.'

19-   <u>**Tim and Kinjo Escape**</u>

'What do you reckon they'll do, Tim?'

'Your - mm - guess is as good as mine. I'd say Robert's a bit - mm - peeved that he didn't capture Tom *and* Ned last night. Here we are - mm - in this big old shed, no easy way of escaping as best I - mm - can figure out and Tom's been taken away - mm - by some thugs, at Robert's request. It's - mm - pretty clear the team of Ned and Tom have - mm - been successful at chasing Restless ones; now the big Boss himself wants to - mm - eliminate *them* once and for all. Makes sense.'

'Well we can't let him, Tim! Let's explore this place, now that it is light. The three doors we can see are locked and maybe guarded outside. They were tough bastards, those men we bumped into here last night. I'd like to clobber that bloke who wacked Brutus with a stick after the dog made a charge at Robert as if he *knew* he was the ringleader.'

'Yeah, that - mm - was interesting. Brutus was being aggressive to all those opposing us, but - mm - when Robert walked through that - mm - green door over there, Brutus was beside himself with fury and flew at him.'

'It was pitch dark when we ran in here, helter skelter behind Tom. Thinking back, that was pretty dumb, eh?'

'Hindsight doesn't - mm - help, Kinjo. Yes, we could have – should have – chosen to - mm - surround this building. As far as we knew, we outnumbered those - mm - running away by maybe three to one. *Then*, we - mm - could have made a controlled entrance ourselves when we could *see* what was what. Yeah, we were stupid - mm - and now we've got to be smarter - mm - to get ourselves out of here. It looks as if nobody has stepped up - mm - to take over from Tom as our leader. Let's try!'

'Good oh, Tim. First, let's chat quietly to everyone here and explain what we hope to do. Until we've tested this prison of ours, we don't want any guards outside to become suspicious.'

'Ok. First - mm - thing is to inspect walls, floor and - mm - ceiling as best we can. There's no ladder in here, but - mm - maybe three or four of us - mm - could hold one man up on our shoulders and I reckon he'd reach the ceiling. There's enough light now - mm - to see what's what.'

Tim and I set about the agreed task. The others soon join in; no one wants to be leader, but all are pleased to be following instructions.

There's a large window in one wall and one skylight in the ceiling, and the three doors. The walls feel solid – concrete panels presumably – and the floor is concrete. No trapdoors or loose blocks there.

The ceiling consists of loose, rectangular sheets of wood or fibreboard. The sheets can be lifted up. The man in the air shoves one aside and is showered in dust for his trouble. The roof cavity is pitch black. It would be some mean task to escape via the roof.

The skylight is then inspected. It consists of a clear panel at ceiling level, a rectangular light-well above and another clear panel in the sloping roof. This latter panel appears to be plastic, not glass, and it is showing signs of disintegrating.

Tim discusses the findings with me and we are surrounded by most of the men, who have been energised out of their previous lethargy.

'The view from the - mm - window suggests this building faces onto a narrow street with - mm - houses or former small businesses on the other side. No - mm - people in sight, which is interesting! We've no idea what's - mm - behind the building, but maybe the green door - mm - leads to other rooms and not to the outside. There's - mm - the door we came through in the dark last night and the other door - mm - might open onto a laneway, or another room.'

Tim continues. 'I think we've - mm - two options. If we could remove or - mm - break through the window, a lot of us - mm - could get out quickly and the others could escape while the - mm - front runners keep the thugs occupied. Alternatively, we could get - mm - one of us into the skylight to remove that - mm - panel in the roof without, with luck, alerting anyone outside.'

'We could do both, Tim. We make ready to bust the window open with, say, 25 of us poised there ready to escape, but before putting that plan into action, the rest of us work to get a couple of blokes out via the skylight to spy the land. If they're detected, we force our way through the window. If they're not detected, we wait to hear what's outside this room and *then* we plan the great escape. It could be that one door is bolted but not guarded and we could bust out that way.'

Clambering through broken window glass is something better avoided, so everyone agrees with my plan.

It doesn't take long for one man to remove the ceiling panel at the skylight and brace himself on its support edge. The panel in the roof is brittle and it almost falls apart when he pushes on it. With care he pokes his head through the hole. There's nobody in sight, but he can only see the side of the building facing the street. With an effort, he raises his body higher and swings a leg out over the roof. Soon he can stand and look about.

Quietly, he walks to one side and looks down. He tells us later that the door on this side was not barred or blocked; he couldn't tell how it was locked. The laneway on that side was uncluttered and there was *nobody* in sight. The green door led to one similar sized room and the final wall, the one without a door, butted up against another building.

'Right, let's attack the side door first.'

Two big men shoulder the door; it splinters and with a

bit more work, a man-sized hole forms. With a cheer, each man scrambles through to the outside.

I look around. 'We're out, but our captors have gone. I suppose they went as soon as they had Tom in their clutches.'

I go to the rear of the building where the other room is. The outer door there is open. I go in, searching for any clues of what Robert's plan might be. I see some blood drops on the floor. These continue outside and down the laneway away from the street, so I call to Tim and soon others are scouting around for more signs. After about 50 metres there's no more blood to be found. This is just before the lane reaches a street; which way now, left or right?

Tim sends ten men left and ten to the right. No clues turn up.

It is not yet mid-morning. Steve says he will head to Government House. He reckons his dog would instinctively go there. If Brutus is not badly injured, he will bring Brutus back because his nose would provide the best means of tracing where Robert went; the intensity with which Brutus attacked when Robert entered the room implied, said Steve, that Robert's odour had been in the Library not long before he and Brutus searched there late yesterday afternoon.

Tim sends five men to Parliament House and the rest of us stay at the building, each person searching for any clues while we all wait for the anticipated arrival of Ned Youd.

20-   <u>A Conundrum</u>

I am still cooling my heels when Helen arrives. Jean could free herself in the afternoon if needed. Brutus is not limping as noticeably, though his leg is still tender. He'll come good if Steve arrives home, she reckons.

Together with the others I discuss what to do. We should return to Patrick Street and try to trace where Tom and the others had gone; most likely, Robert will not be far away from the missing men.

I allow the Bourke sons to remain at their home, and then I move off behind Helen as fast as I can with my band of seven men.

A shout. Rounding a corner come five men; they are just 100 metres away and we soon come up to them.

'We was on our way to tell youse what happened. We just escaped from the building.'

'What building?'

A second man adds, 'We'll go back there now. It's about a kilometre. All of us are searching for clues.'

The first man says, 'They took Tom away this morning.'

'Show us the way.'

Soon, I am there.

'Young fellow, what's your name?'

'Kinjo Yaxley. This is Tim. He's a sheep farmer from Ross.'

'Nice to meet you both. I take it you are Bill Yaxley's son – the Buddhist.'

Kinjo grins, 'When I find the time, I'm trying to persuade Tim to try it.'

Tim explains everything that had happened last night and how the trail of blood only goes so far. The search for more clues had not yielded anything, so Tom's whereabouts remain unknown. Tim sums up, 'Now you - mm - know as much as we do'.

'We don't know whose blood it is, do we Tim. We wounded a few of them last night and Brutus helped too. He *might* have bitten Robert before that big bloke whacked his hind leg and kicked him through the green door. We're afraid, though, that they might have roughed up Tom before taking him away.'

I nod, 'There's no doubt we would be helped a lot if Brutus was here now. I suggest we leave a few of us, say five, at the building while the rest of us spread out behind Helen's horse. If Steve comes back with Brutus, the men can explain where we've gone.'

'Okay, Ned. Let's split in two. We'll need to go a short way up each side street we come to, looking for signs of recent activity.'

'Thanks, Kinjo. Are all Buddhists so clever?'

'Dunno, but Buddhism's main strength is in controlling the mind and I like to think things through.'

'Wait! What Helen said yesterday is still important, I reckon. Robert would be able to hear her horse long before she could see him. I suggest that Helen move well away from here to search the streets on a grid pattern. The rest of us can work as you suggest, Kinjo, but without making a noise. The evidence is plain; Robert will do his work inside buildings, so we will have to inspect any plausible hiding place as we go. Check for door knobs that lack dust, and so on.'

The day progresses; it has threatened to rain, though midday comes and none has fallen. I guess the men have covered all streets within a kilometre to the north, east and west of the building where they'd been held captive.

'Wayne, this needle in a haystack effort is useless. We'll have to be smarter. Let's call a halt for an hour while we try to identify Robert's real hiding place. This could even be south of the building; the trail of blood could have been a ruse – a convenient ruse, perhaps – and Robert would have made sure he and whoever had hold of Tom would disappear *without* trace.'

'I can see your point, Ned. You know, he would only have to have moved three kilometres away, you know, and he had a long head start on us. We'd not, you know, find him in a month of Sundays.'

I ask some men to try to locate the other search team and tell them to return to the building for a planning meeting.

When most of the men have returned, I call for attention: 'Please remain standing. We are all lazy thinkers when we're seated. Anyone with an idea or suggestion should speak up and everyone else should listen.

'Now, I think you can all feel that our search this morning was not likely to succeed. It could have had success *if* Robert had been too lazy to take Tom for more than a short walk. Robert is *neither* stupid *nor* lazy.

'We need to think as Robert thinks. You will say, "I've seen him just once in this room, and he said nothing." Okay, but imagine *you* planned to capture Tom and *you* needed a good place to keep him hidden and *you* are also familiar with the city and have had months, even years, to explore it and to note suitable hiding places. Robert also wants to capture me. He will want to set a trap, perhaps similar to the one he set for Tom, though I'm sure he'd have other options on his mind too.'

There was a low murmur, until one man spoke, spurring others to follow.

'There's the cells at the central police station.'

'Or, at the City Court House; perhaps even at the Supreme Court building across the street from Parliament House.'

'There's also private schools. They're big with many rooms and they're surrounded by open space. A sentry inside a room at each corner of a building would detect our search party, so Robert would have the upper hand if we approached the building.'

Wayne adds his thoughts, 'We're pretty sure, you know, Robert wants to capture, you know, Government House, Parliament House, you know, the electricity distribution centre on Pottery Creek Road and – I surmise – he, you know, has a personal attraction to the main Library building. You know, these and every other building anyone has, you know, talked about would be within three kilometres from where, you know, we are right now, and many of them would be within two k's. If we split up, we could, you know, check a good number before it gets dark.'

A few of the men here live at Government House and have some familiarity with building locations in the old city, but most live elsewhere, like I do, and we'll all be more effective if we know where we are going.

I need a specific plan. I'd need horse riders to maintain contact with each search group so that if one group did make contact with Robert or his men, the word could soon get to the others. Still, it is too pressing to waste the daylight waiting for Helen, so I form search groups, centred in each case on a man who lives at Government House and who can guide his group to a given destination. Four such groups were formed, each with around ten men in them.

'Tim, have you an idea of the total number of men that were involved in fighting and capturing you blokes last night?'

'It is - mm - hard to say, given the darkness and - mm - the state of confusion. We were in the majority at - mm - Patrick Street, but we lost that advantage as soon - mm - as we entered this room, because some of - mm - Robert's men closed the door behind us and the blokes we were - mm - chasing shot through the green door opposite, which they must have - mm - known about, but we were too slow and that door - mm - was closed in our face. I'd - mm - say they might not have numbered more than 25 or 30 all up.'

I turn and address everyone:

'Think twice before entering any building! Any one of our groups is not likely to have a majority, and the enemy will be there, because it suits *them*. Another ambush we don't want. No, if you uncover the hiding place, try to control the exits but *don't* enter. I surmise that Tom will be used in some way to get *me* to rescue him. When I decide to do that, I want to have the balance of numbers on my side, so I'm counting on all of you to be available to help me when the time comes.

'Okay, go check your targets. If there's no sign of Helen, make sure one of you at least is able to report your observations to other groups and report to me too. I'm staying here. I'm also well aware that none, save a few, have had anything to eat or drink for 24 hours or thereabouts. If you can find any food *stop and eat it!*'

One group guide says, 'We sometimes come down from the House and raid what were supermarkets and food shops; potatoes three times a day can be boring. There is still a lot of safe food about. Any tin that still has its original shape is worth opening and there is still stuff in bottles too.'

The room empties. I'm alone and facing *another* waiting time. People imagine farming is a boring task, but it is never like the last week; on my farm there is *always* work to do.

Mid-afternoon; Helen arrives, bringing the rain with her.

'I've not found any sign of Robert or his men, though it's impossible to check everything. I went by the Pottery Creek site, but it looked quiet there.'

'Thanks, Helen. I'd like you to start riding between the four groups now out checking certain buildings. If any group uncovers evidence of Robert, I want all groups plus myself to know quickly.'

Helen says she can find the places mentioned and off she goes.

Alone again! I feel guilty that I am one of the few who'd had a substantial meal last night plus several beers. I go through the green door into the next room. This is almost as big as the main room, but it is not as sparse; some furniture and shop fittings are there. I start opening drawers and cupboard doors. No food of any kind, but I do uncover four scraps of paper – two scraps have three handwritten words on them and two have two words on them. Who's writing? At first, the words make little sense, but if I shuffle the papers I imagine there could be the makings of a story of some sort.

Helen returns; 'Everyone at Government House is as well as can be. Brutus is still sore, but he's running in circles around Steve, so it looks as if no lasting damage was done. Steve said he wouldn't want to be in Robert's shoes or those of the thug who'd whacked Brutus.' She returns to her liaison duties.

I look at the pieces of paper again before putting them in my pocket. I guess the words are a kind of code and I wish Tom was here; it always impresses me what Tom either knows or can figure out. Perhaps staring at carrots has benefits.

It's getting dark and still raining. I don't want to get involved in another night time brawl. Can each group complete its search before the tide turns in Robert's favour? Darkness is Robert's ally.

Darkness is close when the first search group returns. They are convinced their target building is unoccupied. This news does not signify failure. At the planning meeting earlier, a total of ten possible targets had been suggested, so it would not be a disaster if all four teams have been unsuccessful.

So it turns out. It troubles me that Tom will now spend a night as Robert's captive. No doubt – a long night! I call everyone together.

'It is still raining and it's dark – despite the fact there was a full moon two nights ago. It is not a night when you'd expect sentries to be active outside their building. I reckon Robert will feel safe until daylight tomorrow. I have a plan, but I need volunteers and I will accept if none come forward.

'There are six targets still on the list. We have four guides who could find these places in the dark – *I hope*. I suggest that each guide who is willing should take a small number of men, four at most, and make his way to a target. He and his men will inspect the target from all sides, as silently as they can, on the chance they might detect sounds coming from inside the building, which would reveal the hiding place of Robert, his men and of Tom too.

'Each guide will bring his men back here as soon as they can conclude that the interior is silent or that there *are* sounds within. In this way, we can quickly decide if our original list of targets was valuable. What I'd like is that by crack of dawn tomorrow, all of us could be standing outside *one* building ready to break in.'

Soon four groups head outside. A wind has sprung up, making life unpleasant and making it harder to hear sounds in buildings too. Still, we *have* to try something and maybe my plan will turn the darkness to *our* advantage.

It is nigh on impossible to see anything inside the room. One man says he reckons he can get a fire going if anyone has some dry paper to start with. Mention of paper reminds me of the paper scraps in my pocket.

'Kinjo, where are you? Can you find me? I'm near the green door.'

'Coming. Keep talking.'

I do as suggested and soon he collides with me.

'I found some bits of paper in the next room. There's writing on them and my gut feel is that Robert left the papers for us to find. Perhaps it is a trick to lure me into a trap. If we can get some light in here, I'd like you to look at the words.'

There are some fumbling noises in the room and occasional curses as men bump into each other, but then a flicker of light appears. We gather burnable stuff and soon a steady flame is established. There is sufficient wood in the other room to maintain the fire through the night; the smoke can find its way through the broken skylight. Shadows dance along the walls as men move to more comfortable places to await the return of the search parties.

Kinjo and I move nearer to the fire and I give him the papers.

'There are four pieces and you might need to shuffle them to get any sense out of the words.'

Kinjo moves the papers around on the floor. After a while he turns to me.

'Whoever did this reads books, I reckon. These papers make reference to novels, two famous ones at any rate. For instance, look at this one:

… seek him everywhere …

'At school our teacher told us about *The Scarlet Pimpernel*. It's a famous novel about the French Revolution; the Pimpernel was the nickname of an Englishman who was trying to protect French aristocrats from being guillotined by the revolutionaries, who were trying to take over control from the upper class. The teacher had us remember these lines:

> "They seek him here, they seek him there, those French-
> ies seek him everywhere.
> Is he in heaven or is he in hell?
> That damned elusive Pimpernel."

'She explained that the novel was written about 250 years ago, so it was an early indication that whoever is in control of a country should ensure the majority of people could have a *real* say in the running of the country. She used the story to emphasise to us the *value* of our island culture, where we can direct our own lives, thanks to our Clan Members and the Assembly. To me, these words indicate that the writer sees himself as a current-day Scarlet Pimpernel, seeking to secure a return to power by the one-time ruling class.'

'That's Robert, isn't it!'

'Yes, Ned, it fits; Wayne said Robert likes the Library here.'

Kinjo's revelations buoy me up; we are onto something *at last*.

'What's the other novel?'

'There's a hidden meaning in this one too:

… uncle … cabin …

'I'm pretty sure these words refer to an even more famous novel, written at least 300 years ago, about slavery in America. The book's title was *Uncle Tom's Cabin*, hence these words hint at Tom being where Robert is.'

'*Ah, hah!* This shows that Robert wrote these words *after* he'd captured just one of us. These papers must comprise the trail Robert decided to leave to get *me* into his clutches. He was stringing a long bow, though, wasn't he? I mean, he could not have known you were in our group. Who else could have known what you've just told me?'

'Speaking as a novice Buddhist, I can surmise two reasons. First, he believes he is intellectually superior to the mass of islanders – us – and couldn't resist leaving this demonstration of his knowledge. Secondly, both these novels depict scenes that Robert could think have relevance today. Tom was a Negro slave in America, thus the lowest of low class. Although the novel presents a sympathetic portrait of Tom, I guess Robert is implying that Tom Badcock is no better than a slave. Perhaps Robert is signalling that he will make an example of Tom; anyone who *resists* the Restless culture will become a slave. You'd be one too.'

'And you, Kinjo! Any more clues in the words?'

'These words might hint at another novel, but I can't guess what it would be.'

… Clue … Diary …

I stand and say to the room, 'Do these words mean anything to anyone: "Clue, Diary"?' There's no response.

'And, the last scrap?'

'I left this to last as the words are well-known, I think:

… red all over …

They are part of a trick question that children would ask each other 200 or more years ago. The full question goes, "What is black and white and read all over?" The catch is in the confusion created by the words "red" r-e-d and "read" r-e-a-d sounding the same when the question is *spoken*.'

'The answer?'

'The answer is a newspaper, although I guess Robert might have been thinking of books instead, given his apparent interest in the Library.'

'*Hmmm.* Steve and Brutus searched the Library yesterday and Steve concluded that somebody had been there recently. I think you are on the right track, so thanks Kinjo.'

It is now clear that our attempt to check those buildings on our list is not going to be a fruitful one. Whichever group returns first should go out and do a similar check of the Library. This had been the last of the ten we'd listed!

What are the implications of Kinjo's explanation? Is Robert prepared for me to enter the Library surrounded by 40 islanders? Unlikely! Does he have sufficient support to match my men? Also unlikely, though a well-constructed defence could swing the balance his way. Could he somehow close the exits so we are all locked in? Could this be to his advantage? It *would* allow him to proceed to occupy *his* key targets with the certainty of minimal opposition.

What if we enter the building and find Tom standing on a chair with a noose around his neck and Robert calls for me to come forward on my own? That's a tough one!

Perhaps it would be smarter if I were to arrange my men at entrance doors, ready to burst in at sound of conflict, while I go inside on my own and do as Robert requests at least until I can size up the whole situation. The more I think of this option, the more it appeals, because it avoids risking the loss of my supporting force before we have understood Robert's intentions.

Cont'd →

141

21-   <u>Closing In</u>

The men return from checking the Library: 'We can't be sure, Ned. It's a large building and it does seem that the ground floor is unoccupied, but people could be upstairs and we'd not hear them unless they set out to *make* a noise. The building is located on the side of a steep hill and it would have been simple to create a basement floor there by digging out part of the hillside.'

Robert is proving it easy to be a modern-day Scarlet Pimpernel! Surely he *has* to be in the Library, with Tom there too, but there is that puzzling clue. I turn to Kinjo.

'That riddle was for a newspaper. I want to think more about that. The island hasn't had any newspapers for more than 80 years. One newspaper used to be published in the old city, but it shut down soon after the collapse, because the people involved had to leave in search of food. It might have appeared on and off for a couple of years, but the islanders showed they weren't much interested; besides, a couple of competing papers did continue publication elsewhere for a decade or so and these did not have the taint of the Restless culture like the city paper did. What do *you* think?'

'Well, assuming that building still stands, it could be the location intended by Robert. It *was* a newspaper company's building, even if there isn't a single paper there now. That company would have promoted the Restless culture; many of the paper's readers would have benefitted most from that culture, at least from the politics centred here in the city and the building could even be one of Robert's key targets. If he can establish a stronghold for the Restless ones, he would need a way to spread propaganda.'

'You know, the more you talk, the more I'm inclined to take lessons in Buddhism from you.'

I ask if anyone knows where the old newspaper building is located.

'It's still standing and not far away', says one man, but another man interjects, 'You're talking of the original headquarters, which became a heritage listed building, but the printing works moved to a new area near the Bowen bridge well before the collapse of the Restless culture.'

I realise that I might have seen that particular building when I went to check on the sentries at Bowen – when was it – three days ago. It looked large, but only had a ground floor, I think. It meant nothing to me, but *now* it occurs to me that maybe it is one reason why Nigel and his band had been told to occupy the grandstand at Elwick, which is but a few minutes' walk from this "new" newspaper building. While we have been chasing Robert nearer the centre of the city, Nigel could have occupied the printing works and encountering *no* opposition!

I decide to check on the original newspaper building if the Library proves to be empty. I can now see the street through the window and I doubt we could inspect the original building without being detected, but perhaps this isn't an issue any longer. If Robert isn't in the Library, we can soon relocate and I can go in with the same plan. If it proves to be unoccupied, it would seem I'll have no option but to make the seven kilometre trek to Elwick.

Time to move camp. I am sick of the building we've been in and I'm sure everyone else is as well; even more so. The rain has gone, but it is not warm, because a cold south-west wind is troubling everyone.

I appoint door marshals, as I call them, to oversee the men placed at each door to the Library. Their task is to be alert to any noise of a fight inside or of me calling for help. I see no problem in their being a few metres inside the building; this will give them a better chance of grasping what is happening, yet still be in contact with the men outside.

I go to what I'm told was once the main door. Originally comprising two glass doors sliding on runners, now there is but one door, motionless. I walk in and look around. A staircase is in front of me. There is no welcoming party.

I start to climb the stairs, and I ask a man to follow me yet remain one floor behind. Through an internal wall of glass on the first floor, I can see shelf after shelf of books, but no person appears. I move up one more floor; this has a similar design. Again, nobody appears.

'Hullo there! Is anyone home?' Silence!

What does this mean? Is the Library unoccupied or am I being lured further in to a trap set by Robert? If the latter, I decide to call the bluff and begin to speak as loud as I can, 'Well, there's nobody here, men, so let's go to the next building.' I descend to the entrance. Nobody follows me.

It is not long at all before I stand outside the newspaper building. We've no time to locate all access doors, so I take a chance. All my men congregate outside what was the main entrance. We need to force this door open, implying that nobody had gone in before us and this turns out to be the case. I check the first two floors, but encounter silence, and *dust*. It seems nobody has been inside for *decades!* I shout my intention to depart, but nobody comes forth.

Bugger! I stand on the front steps and look at the men.

'You have gone well beyond any call for duty and you could all have expected to be on your way home by this time. I am loath to ask you to follow me to Elwick. I release every one of you from any continued duty to me. I will head north now on my way to harass Robert to the best of my ability and to rescue Tom.'

The men are agitated by this unwanted turn of events. Then Tim speaks.

'Ned, none of us - mm - want to give up, I'm sure. After all, without - mm - you and Tom opposing Robert, it is pretty clear he would - mm - already have secured his many initial objectives in the - mm - city and the momentum this would have - mm - given him would make it much more difficult for anyone to - mm - oppose him successfully. We all need *both* of you - mm - fighting for us.

'For my part - mm - I will head to Elwick with you. It *is* on the route I - mm - would take to go home to Ross, so I will delay any decision to - mm - walk away from this campaign until I've helped you check on the printing works.'

Tim's speech swings the crowd around to a consensus. The vast majority of the men come from places north of Bridgewater, so Tim's intention becomes their intention too. The men who live at Government House have a different perspective, but what one of them says pleases me no end.

'Ned, we're indebted to you already for saving our House from being overrun and we believe Robert must still have the House in his sights. We will go home now, and see if we can persuade others to head to Elwick with us. With luck, we won't be far behind you, with a crowd.'

I've not done much walking the last three days and it is good to get the legs working. I doubt it will rain today. The wind is persistent, but now it is blowing from behind, so it does not feel as cold.

One worrying thought occurs as we walk along; I am removing all my available men away from the old city centre on the assumption I will need them to overwhelm Robert's Force, or what remains of it, but is this part of Robert's plan? He wouldn't need all his men, if he has set up Tom such that I'll be forced to let go *my* men to save my mate's life. If so, Robert could have left many of his own men in the city and they could attack his intended targets with a reasonable impunity. By the end of today, he could thereby have captured both Tom *and* me *and* have secured some or all of his key targets.

I put this possible situation to Kinjo and Tim. Tim is first to comment.

'It's - mm - plausible alright, though I don't - mm - think you've much option to what you're doing now. A weakness we've - mm - had is being split into several groups, not - mm - knowing if each group would be needed at any one time. Instead - mm - you now have your whole force dedicated to one - mm - objective. It's a gamble you have to take.'

'Yes, Ned, Tim's right. If we find there's nobody at the printing works, you can race back to the centre and search for the Force. On the other hand, if Robert is where we think he is, we will have the opportunity to capture *him* and I reckon if we do that, it won't much matter if his Force does capture some buildings. Without Robert to lead them, the Force won't be a force for long and we can drive them out in a day or two.'

Wayne had been following us and he voices his assessment. 'I think Kinjo, you know, is correct. These extra men that Robert somehow found are not known to me, but, you know, it would surprise me if they were a force in their own right. I'm more sure that Robert co-opted them, you know, with the promise of some reward. If we capture Robert, you know, there'd be precious little chance of a reward eventuating.'

All this leads me to try and plan how to tackle the printing works. I don't recall seeing any windows, but I could only see one side of the building from the bridge access road and this could have been the backside. However, it might be possible to conceal the majority of my men from anyone inside the building, so Robert could not be sure where my main force is. I even had "form" as that old saying goes. Tim was correct; we had always split our force, so why wouldn't I do so now as well?

Two welcome sounds interrupt my train of thought. Bruce and his whip and Steve with Brutus were closing in on us and with them come eight others from Government House. *Now,* I have some real options!

Bruce catches up and says, 'We've arranged for Helen

and Jean to watch our House and the Bourke's too. At the sign of anybody attacking those places, the girls will ride here to let you know.'

I think I now have a workable plan of attack, though Kinjo has a further thought.

'Those paper scraps you found look more sinister now. It could be that Robert wants you to focus on saving Tom instead of defending the targets in the city centre. The risk is that we will find Tom is in the Elwick building, held captive by Nigel, but Robert will not be in the building. Robert's had a day and a night to arrange all this.'

22-   <u>**Electrocuted in One Hour**</u>

I approach the printing works at a fast walk; I want it to seem that I am determined. With me I have Tim, Kinjo and Bruce – his whip can signal the others to come running from their hiding place. I asked Steve to keep a bit further away in case the sound of Brutus' barking alerts those inside the building to the presence of more of my men.

There are several floor-to-ceiling glass panels at the front, but some of them are broken now and we step through one gap and find an inside door, which is open. Light shines through a row of small glass windows high up on the wall to my left. Nobody in sight!

'Hello there. Is anyone at home?'

A scuffling sound makes me glance to my left – a rat?

'It's taken you a while to find me, Edward.'

I look right and Robert appears from behind a large reel of paper.

'Where's Tom, you bastard?'

'Now, let's be civil shall we? I'll take you to Thomas after you've told your men to leave this building.'

I turn to my men. 'Go as far as the glass wall, but no further.'

I note that Robert's right hand is bandaged. Has Brutus bitten him? Inwardly, I am pleased. Brutus might soon have a second chance.

'Lead on,' I say.

We enter a large room, packed with machinery, so it isn't possible to see much of the opposite wall. Robert leads me around the end of one machine.

Several men, maybe ten stand looking at me and in the middle is Tom bound to a chair with rope, his mouth gagged.

'What the hell have you done?'

'It was the only way to shut him up. He drove us mad with all his chatter. How do you tolerate that, Edward?'

'I don't respond. Besides, he's my mate. If I told him to shut up for whatever reason he'd just talk more. The thing is Bob, Tom does make a lot of sense in with all his palaver. That is, if you have a mind to hear it.'

'I'm Robert.'

'Get off your *fu-kn* soap box, Bob. You come over all nice and polite, formal and all that, but that is an act pure and simple. A fellow in my group is more than forty years younger than me, but somehow he knows a lot more than I do about what life was like two or three hundred years ago. He said there was a book or a movie called *The Godfather*, about the boss of a ruthless criminal gang. Apparently, this bloke always dressed neatly, never raised his voice or showed emotion, cold as a fish, but he had his thugs commit murders. To put it bluntly, the Godfather was the most evil bastard of the lot. And, that's *you* now, isn't it?'

I detect the hint of a smile on Robert's face.

'Untie my mate now!'

'I will not accede to your blunt demand, Edward. You see, in about one hour my men at the electricity distribution centre will close a circuit breaker and inhabitants of this building will once again enjoy the benefits of electricity; that is, except Thomas, who is wired to the high-voltage circuit that once enabled these giant printing presses to operate twenty four hours a day. Thomas will not enjoy the experience, but so what; one less farmer on the island will be neither here nor there.

'Speaking of which, I have another chair and it's ready for you to sit on. Please be my guest.'

'One hour, you said?'

'Yes. Clocks *do* have their uses, you know.'

'And will you be watching the fireworks display in here,

then?'

'Oh no, my men and I have much more important work to do in the city. Your late arrival here has delayed our departure, though my plan is flexible and we'll still secure all the targets sometime today.'

The men step aside, revealing the second chair. Against two, I might stand a chance, but not against ten. The gang surges forward.

'Stand back, I'm armed,' I shout, moving my right hand inside my jacket. The two closest men hesitate, but the others swarm around both sides and pin my arms behind me. They waste no time in tying me to the chair and in making sure the electric wires make contact with my legs as well.

'You bastards,' I shout as loud as I can. Did Tim and the others hear me? I decide not to say anything more in case I am rendered silent in the same way Tom had been.

Having done their work to Robert's satisfaction, he and the gang make moves to depart. It makes sense to Robert, I guess, to leave the scene in case some of my men come looking for me. With luck, he is aware only of the three who'd followed me into the building and my men will overpower Robert's gang so they won't get to do their work. He heads around the machine and out of sight. I shout, 'good riddance', as much to satisfy myself as to alert my men.

The sound of a fight comes to my ears and the unmistakeable *crac*k of Bruce's whip. Will Tim tear himself away and come looking for me as planned?

'Tim, I'm up this end of the building, behind the machine.'

A short while later, I repeat what I'd said. The noise outside continues, then:

'Ned, Tom, where are you?' It's Kinjo. I repeat my instructions and soon his face appears.

'Kinjo! There isn't much time. Try first to remove the

wires from my legs and from Tom's legs. They're not live now, but will be in some minutes.'

He kneels behind me and I can hear him breathing rapidly.

'Sorry, I'm fumbling too much and can't get a good grip.'

'Stop, take two deep breaths and start again *slowly* – more haste means less speed, don't you know.'

Soon Kinjo moves to Tom's chair and it isn't long before Tom is also out of danger. Next, Kinjo removes the rags from around Tom's head.

'Bloody oath, Ned. What took you so long? I've been trussed up like this for over a day!'

'So, we're equal now, are we?'

'Yes, I'll never mention your wet pants anymore.'

'Shall I tell him all the searching we did before we got here?'

'Not now, Kinjo, but I will say, Tom, that without Kinjo's wisdom, you'd soon be grilled meat.'

Kinjo undoes the last knots and Tom can stand – rather, he *tries* to stand up, but his legs cramp and he plonks himself back on the chair and sighs. Gradually, he regains his composure.

'Did you really infuriate Robert?'

'Yes. I began as you did by accusing him and the others for being criminals and gangsters. It seemed to me that, whatever I said, they'd heard it all before. I guessed I was wasting my breath and my time for no result, so I changed and began talking about whatever came into my head. Eventually, I hit on nursery rhymes. It was after I'd sung *Twinkle, Twinkle Little Star* and alternated that with *Mairzy Doats* for about six times, that Robert did his block and told one bloke to tie my head up tight.'

'You're tone deaf, you are.'

'Yeah, pretty effective I reckon.'

'I'd like to hear your story of what happened from when

you reached the fight on Patrick Street, but not now. If you can stand, let's go outside and view the damage.'

Noise of the fight has dissipated by the time we step through the gap in the glass wall. My men are holding several of the gang who'd tied me up.

'How many?'

'Seven so far, but we're chasing the rest. I don't reckon they'll get far, because Steve will let Brutus loose.'

'Any injuries?'

'Nothing too serious this time. They weren't using iron bars and stakes – must have figured we'd not be so close.'

I notice Wayne off to one side and I ask him to stand beside me. His eyes still show evidence of the battering he'd endured two days ago, but he can now see pretty well. I go to the nearest one of the gang and look him in the eye.

'Where are you from?'

'Yingina.'

'Why are you supporting Robert?'

'He's a good bloke.'

'And us islanders are not, are you saying? What were you doing in Yingina?'

'Staring at four walls.'

'What were you in for?'

'Murder.'

'So, Robert sprung you out of gaol, did he?'

'Yeah, that's right.'

'Were your mates in that building also escaped criminals?'

'Dunno … Robert wanted us to focus on the job.'

This bloke is trying my patience.

'Such as to electrocute two innocent farmers.'

'You opposed his plans.'

'Two more murders were nothing to you, then?'

'Nah, I was out of gaol … that's all that mattered.'

'Were you the bastard who kicked Brutus, the dog, two nights ago?'

'I couldn't see who did it.'

'Well, I'm going to make sure Brutus can settle that score. Did you ever stop to think what would happen to you once Robert was in control of the old city?'

'Nah, I might not be part of it.'

'I can assure you and your mates that Robert doesn't care a fig for you. You're all expendable. Just as Tom and I weren't part of his grand plan, he will have already planned a way to get rid of you too. If any of you have any sense and find yourselves free, clear out of this city and go hide somewhere. There is *no* future in murder and thuggery, and *no* future in following Robert either. Got that?'

Wayne enters the conversation. 'Ned's right, I was a follower, but I realised Robert has his own agenda, you know, and I doubted I would be part of it; he couldn't provide for me what I needed.'

I ask, 'Where were you and Robert heading?'

'Pottery Creek Road, he said.'

'To do what?'

'Meet his Force.'

I want to free up as many of my men as I can, so we can get back to the city centre and combat Robert. I tell a couple of my men to use ropes and electric cables from the printing works to tie these latest captives together at ankle level. That way, they can only walk if everyone mimics what his neighbour is doing and any out-of-step move will bring the lot of them down to the ground.

The result provides great comic relief. One of my men ties their hands too, but in a different order; left hand of first man to right hand of third man, second to fourth, and so on. Hence, when they trip over each other, it requires a level of coordination and cooperation, beyond their capability to get back on their feet. Not surprising, really; most criminals are not known for their intelligence, to say nothing about their lack of tolerance towards other human beings. "Honour among thieves" is only found in novels. The air is soon thick with crude curses.

All this takes a half hour or so. I search their pockets and remove the knives there and then we speed off around an inlet from the Derwent River, before turning south-west.

Cont'd 

23-   <u>Brutus Catches the Big Fish</u>

Not long after, we come upon an excited group. Bruce, Steve and several others have formed a circle and inside stand three men, looking scared. Brutus, crouching with head low to the ground, is walking slowly sideways around the men and watching them as if they are cattle. Steve comes to me:

'I didn't see Robert. Somewhere between the printing works and where I was hiding with Brutus, he must have split from these three. He *is* a smart bugger!'

Bruce adds, 'I broke away from the first fight as soon as your reserve force was close enough to take over. I ran after Robert and these blokes. They were a way ahead and I did not see how, but Robert got away. He might be smart, but I'd add he's a bloody lucky bastard too.'

'*Damn!*' I call for attention.

'Some of you stay and find a way to make sure this gang can't get away, then head to Government House as fast as you can, 'cos Robert intends to attack it today. The rest of you split into two groups. One group, go straight away to Parliament House. I don't care about the building, but the Bourke family deserve all the help we can give them.

'The last group will come with me. I want Kinjo, Tim and Wayne in this group, please. Steve can lead us back towards the printing works to see if Brutus can pick up Robert's scent. He'll be on his own and he knows his way around this city; I reckon he'll head to Pottery Creek Road, so if we can't find a trace of him, that's where we'll head too. Okay?'

Brutus dashes here and there, but doesn't seem to be following any scent. We reach the seven "amigos" struggling to stand up after stumbling to the ground yet again. Suddenly, Brutus runs straight at one of the men and sinks his teeth in the bloke's leg. All seven collapse in a pile again. Steve grabs his dog's collar and drags him away. I step forward and punch that bloke in the jaw. Knocked out cold, he will be a dead weight for a while. I reckon this magnificent seven could benefit from learning yet more teamwork, so we leave them and head south again.

This time, Brutus finds something interesting and branches off to the right. Head down, he moves at speed and we struggle to keep up. We don't want to stop him while he is in this mood.

After about a kilometre, Brutus stops. Steve says, 'Looks as if he's lost the scent.'

I've been so keen to keep up with Brutus that I need to ask, 'Where are we?'

Steve replies, 'We've reached Moonah. We'd be about a kilometre north of the Moonah shopping street and we're heading more or less toward the Pottery Creek area.'

'Before we go there, let's walk Brutus around in the hope that he can pick up the scent again.'

We spend a few minutes going to the left and the right. To me, this is odd.

'I dunno, but Brutus appeared to be sure of the trace he was following, and then stop! How could Robert give him the slip?'

Tom has regained his voice.

'Could he have changed his clothes or sprayed himself with some strong-smelling liquid? Would this confuse Brutus?'

Kinjo remarks, 'That would mean Robert had to suspect he would be followed by a dog, hence he planted his means of escape here beforehand. Could he be so smart?'

Tim suggests, 'Maybe he - mm - doubled back along the way he'd - mm - come for a while before branching away. Brutus might not - mm - have detected that the scent at just one point was evident in two directions and he - mm - kept going in the one direction.'

I am frustrated. As far as we know, the place to find Robert is Pottery Creek Road, but what if we race there and he's *not* there?

'Tim and Steve, you two and Brutus keep searching around here for twenty minutes more. If you get a new lead, Tim can chase after us; if not, you'd better come to the Pottery Creek centre.'

The rest of us head off down a street. We come to the disused railway line and I know where we are. It isn't long before we are back at the place where I'd waited for Tom to catch up to me two long days ago.

We start walking along Pottery Creek Road. There are fifteen of us. I'd have liked more, but I'd *had* to divide my force yet again. I don't know, of course, if Robert could have factored this problem of mine in his plan, but I was now at the point of believing he *could* have. Naturally, only *he* knew which locations he'd strike at and in which order; I'd be always playing catch-up with ever-weakening strength.

Near the lines of tall electricity pylons, I turn to my men.

'I want to get an understanding of what we're up against before I commit our whole force, such as it is. Wayne and I will enter the buildings. The rest of you keep together. If there's a need for a leader while I'm away, I nominate Kinjo. For Tom's benefit, Kinjo's young, but he's got initiative and a good brain. Listen to what he says. Your bull-headed rush from Patrick Street got you and many others into a lot of trouble and you're lucky that Kinjo has a cool head. Come after us if you sense we're in trouble or if we don't appear in ten minutes or so; we might have to search all the buildings.'

No sign of anybody. The main door of the nearest building is open, so we step inside.

'Hullo there. Is anyone home?' Silence! I check a few of the rooms and it seems there *is* nobody home.

We walk to the next building. Half way there, Wayne says quietly, 'Someone peeped through the window on the left.'

I open the door, step inside and am jumped on by three men. Wayne comes to my aid and for a short while we have a real fight on our hands, until we back out of that building.

None of the three follow us. We look at each other. 'Perhaps they are, you know, the only ones at home and their job is to guard whatever is in that building.'

'Maybe the circuit breakers are in here, Wayne. Let's try the third building before I call up our men and we invade this building.'

We walk around the second building and have almost reached the last one when there is a shout from behind. It is Kin-jo.

'Tim's just arrived. Brutus is on the trail again and it leads away from here.'

'Come on Wayne, we might have the big fish on our hook again. I don't want to lose him this time.'

Tim is still recovering his breath when we reach him.

'Just as I guessed, Ned, he - mm - found the scent some 200 metres back from where he'd lost it. Robert - mm - headed east and Brutus seems - mm - to be dead sure of it.'

'Everyone follow me; we're going back to Steve. Can you manage a fast walk, Tim?'

'I'll - mm - do my best. I'm not as young - mm - as I once was, you know.'

We soon see Steve up ahead and he points away from us.

Once more, we hurry along. The new trail is starting to look more south-easterly, yet I can't be certain about Robert's intended destination. It's not easy to keep up with a very excited dog! Robert would have about two hours start on us, I guess. With luck, we'll catch him before he succeeds in some part of his plan.

Tom says, '*Hej*, Ned. We're just passing that open area

where we stopped three nights ago and it rained.'

I am too busy to comment. Brutus doesn't stop, just turns down one street after another, nose to the ground at all times. What might be going through his mind? Had he managed to bite Robert two nights ago? Was he intent on biting him again?

'Kinjo, does Buddhism give you the ability to read a dog's mind?'

'Not particularly, but I believe if you treat a dog properly, it will find a way to show what its thinking.'

We come to what had been a wide road and turn to follow it. We descend a hill and in front of us there is another hill; this would be the northern end of the Domain. Was Robert heading for Government House? If so, he could be there now.

At the low point between the hills, there are streets and paths heading off in all directions. Brutus turns left off the main road and moves along something like a walking track; it is narrow with several turns in it and it is pretty much overgrown now – maybe it had been a minor road before the collapse, but I don't have time to look at whatever scenery might be in this area. If anything, Brutus has upped his pace. Is the scent getting stronger; are we gaining on Robert? I try to look ahead, in case we come up on Robert unexpectedly, but this isn't easy, as there are stones and roots to trip over if I'm not also watching the ground. Brutus, I say silently; please take pity on us old humans!

There are a few ways to get to the top of the Domain hill. We could clamber up the hill through the trees; this'd be the shortest way, but might not be the quickest route. Luckily Brutus is keeping to roads or paths created sometime before the collapse. We start hugging the right bank of the river; the Domain is on our right, but we have yet to head up the slope.

We come to what had been an intersection; I can see a way of climbing the hill by a path leading towards Government House. Brutus, though, runs straight on, without hesitating, so I begin to realise Robert was not aiming to go there. By continuing, we'll come to the southern bridge; the one Robert came over two days ago with his mob.

We follow Brutus as best we can; the going is much better than it had been a few minutes ago, but Brutus is really running now and he's a good hundred metres in front of us.

The dog turns left onto the bridge approach. Steve is the first of us to reach the turning point and he exclaims, 'Robert's up ahead, near the top of the bridge arch. It looks as if he's stopped.'

Sure enough, Robert is standing and gazing over the bridge railing, oblivious to our approach. I dare not call out, but Brutus barks and leaps ahead at a double gallop. None of us could have stopped him, the way he's going, and we can only look on as the distance between the two of them closes quickly.

Robert starts to climb the railing, but Brutus is too quick, grabs a trouser leg and drags Robert back onto the bridge surface, biting the hand Robert puts up to protect his face.

'Brutus, stop. *Stop!*'

Steve reaches the two of them and grabs his dog's collar. Brutus continues his frenzied barking, until Steve says, 'good boy; *good* dog. Stop him getting away.'

The barking is replaced by a low growling rumble. Brutus starts to walk sideways around the prostrate Robert in the same way I'd seen him do with the three thugs an hour or so ago.

Phew! We begin to recover our breath. Robert appears exhausted; perhaps tired of life. He's found things didn't go as planned. There will be no way now to maintain the face he's shown everyone over the past decade or more.

I step forward.

'Well, Dick Loone, your game is up. Your "Robert" is a failure, but what drove you to even *imagine* you could carry this plan through?'

24-   __Robert Reveals All__

Robert is silent for a good while. The only sound comes from Brutus; growling, he maintains his circular motion around the prostrate body. The rest of us stand watching in silence.

Finally, Steve says, 'Stop, Brutus. Good boy. Let him up.'

Robert turns and sits with his back to the railing.

'It's a long story.'

'I think we have the time, even though my men are all bloody hungry – and that includes Brutus, I'm sure. Tom and I have wasted over three weeks chasing you and your Force and most of my men have spent close on two weeks away from their farms helping us. I think we *deserve* to know how all this came about.'

Robert draws a deep breath, or maybe it is a sigh, and begins to speak.

'I take full responsibility, but if I was to start from the beginning, the urge to restore what you islanders call the Restless culture originated with my mother.

'A strong-willed woman, Mother never stopped talking of how good the life was before the collapse. I've surmised from her lecturing me, when I was a young boy, that it must have been her parents who instilled in her the belief in the Restless culture. I recall meeting my grandparents only briefly and only a couple of times. They treated me as their grandchild and I never gained an inkling of their real feelings, which they may have kept for when they were alone with Mother.

'In me, Mother saw the means of restoring the "good old days".

'My grandparents lived in Sandy Bay, the most affluent suburb. I suspect that my grandfather never worked, I mean *toiled*, though he probably had an office in the city. They had to leave Sandy Bay in a hurry when the collapse came and they found it a struggle – a huge come-down, I guess – and from that experience could have come Mother's dislike, bordering on hatred, of rural people.

'It was ironic; Mother married a farmer. Graeme Loone had a good farm and that's where I lived for about five years. I loved it, but had to keep this to myself, because Mother saw nothing but negatives in farm life. Finally, she left my father and we moved closer to the would-be northern capital – as you call it – and that's where I grew up and finished my schooling.'

I interrupt with one question: 'I've gathered that you see farmers as worthless and expendable. What happened to your father?'

'The separation hit him hard, I think. He sold the farm and moved into a town where he could spend his days in the pub, until his money ran out. He had a brother who took care of him, but he didn't last long unfortunately.'

'It sounds as if you at least had *some* sympathy for *one* farmer.'

'Yes, I hate to admit it, but it's true that my disdain for farmers is due to Mother's influence. I guess I was a "mother's boy", but not in the usual sense. It was just that I felt I had no option but to be aggressive in living my life such that I could fulfil her desire for a re-born Restless culture.

'In the end, I devised the scheme that you learned of those few weeks ago. I felt I was providing a benefit – a means of escape if you will – for those among us who, like Mother, had a longing for some aspects of that culture, which were absent from the islanders' culture. The meetings I arranged were well attended and I feel these people went away contented each time.'

'You could have stayed with that concept, I guess. I mean, by the time you'd set up that meeting format, your mother was no longer alive, was she?'

'True. I'd told her of my plan to create the means for like-minded people to meet without islanders waking up to what was happening. It took a few years to put the plan into action and she passed away during that time.'

So far, everything he'd said had some plausibility.

'I'm still puzzled why you extended your plan to the point where you called a special meeting in May to form your Force.'

'Many of those who came to my meetings expressed a longing for a return of the Restless culture to the island. I came to the view that the last support I could offer them was to *try* to bring this about. I told them at the meeting you referred to, and Wayne will bear me out I hope, that once the Force had gained control of certain key targets in the old city, I would withdraw and where the people took this foothold would be up to them.'

Wayne nods his head.

'Along the way, you set up a callous scheme to electrocute Tom and me. Was that a feature of your mother's view of what's right in the world?'

'In the plan I started with, I was going to capture you two, get you into the printing works and connect you to those wires. That went to plan, though it took more than a day longer than I'd imagined. With my commandoes – as I called them – I would then go directly to the Pottery Creek centre, where I would instruct the men I had kept there to close the circuit breakers. Yes, you would have been electrocuted.

'With you out of the way, my commandoes and I would quickly gain control of two of my original targets. I imagined that it would take a fair while for islanders to dislodge us and I'd have a chance to appeal to the Members at Campbell Town to allow us to *retain* control.'

'My God! You *are* a cold bugger. The reference to the Godfather is spot on isn't it?'

I'm amazed that Tom hasn't uttered a word so far. 'You'll

note, Robert that contact with you has rendered Thomas mute. There are many of us who'll thank you for that.'

This had the effect I sought.

'Ned's right you bastard. I enjoyed making you angry. Other people just let my prattle wash over them, but you bit the bait, you did. Hilarious! I'm silent now, because I'm speechless at your cold-blooded audacity. One point of view would have you being kind to those you tried to help by organising those meetings, but the reverse is that you then fooled a goodly number of them to join your Force. These people had a snowflake's chance in Hell of succeeding; they'll be revealed to us islanders as gullible fools – dangerous fools – because they did not have the common sense to say "No" to a scheme aimed at ultimate subjection of islanders and of our culture.

'You knew your Force was all bluff, didn't you. They were good for occupying places that other people captured on their behalf; that's why you arranged for some nasty criminals to escape from their prisons. Those blokes weren't clever and you exploited this too; they'd thank you for setting them free, but by the time our forces manage to capture them again, they are going to have an even longer list of crimes to answer for. Serious crimes, like working to install the Restless culture on our island – that's akin to treason in our eyes – and they'd be accomplices to two murders!'

Kinjo spots an opportunity to add his penny's worth.

'Though you haven't said so, I reckon that you are an only child and – I suspect – so was your mother. Hence, the intense hurt of your grandparents was focused on indoctrination of their *sole* hope, their daughter. Your mother then passed this task onto *her* only hope. In both instances, your mother and you had a sheltered upbringing; the two of you could not experience the rough and tumble of a life lived among others of similar ages. In your case, your experience came from a life of books, from fiction.

'I reckon you saw yourself as a current-day Pimpernel, but while endeavouring to live that life, you ended up in the shoes of the Godfather. Okay, you didn't *succeed* in the murder of Ned and Tom, but the Force's members and the escaped criminals are well and truly on the sacrificial altar. You *put* them there.'

I have to add to what Kinjo just said.

'I'd like to know how you view Nigel. We've been told he's a "Daddy's boy". If so, it would seem that you tried to lumber onto Nigel the task of helping you to extract redress for your grandparents' hurt. Is he such a disappointment to you that you were willing to have him also lumbered with the charge of treason?'

For a while, it looks as if Robert will not utter another word. When he does, it is to make a startling admission.

'First, I want to explain why I had Nigel trick you into visiting Camp 21. I imagine you have puzzled about that. Make of this what you will, but my intent was to give you two a chance to back off and not pursue me and the others. If you'd heeded the warning I gave you when Wayne freed you from that chain, I would not have needed to carry out your kidnapping and murder.

'Nigel is no more. Yesterday, he killed himself. The members of the Force in his charge had been drifting away and going home. He was left with just five and he saw this as an abject failure on his part.

'If I'd captured you when I captured Thomas, things would have been "on schedule" and I believe I could have influenced Nigel to remain with me. His death weighed heavily on me these last hours. I did not sleep last night and I resolved to not live through another night. I was going to try to capture the targets on my list, at least some of them, but your men grabbed all my commandoes, as I called them, straight after we left the printing works.

'There was no longer any hope for my plan and I headed

here to kill myself. If it wasn't for that confounded dog, I'd be dead now. I *should* be dead. Can you all just walk back to the shore and leave me alone, please?'

'Kinjo, remind me - mm - of what you said at Bridgewater about - mm - Buddhist belief?'

'You mean, Tim, that it's a man's own mind, not his enemy that lures him into evil ways?'

'Yes, that's - mm - true, I see now.'

<u>Afterword</u>

July 20, 2150:

Loone's trial was held at Campbell Town and attended by all fifteen Members and many of the Clan Elders.

Loone had the hide to claim that he was of two minds in leading his gang. He wanted to establish a foothold from where his followers could seek to achieve their own aims, yet he wasn't concerned that his campaign might fail – because, he claimed, he would have awakened the islanders to the realisation that they *had* to protect their own culture. I felt that Tom and I had received strong support from other islanders, though I was disappointed that the constabulary showed no interest. In the end, that was not a problem, but it could well *have* been.

The evidence did support a charge of treason, the judge said, however he felt the suicide of Loone's son was a substantial penalty and, for this charge, he sentenced Loone to spend three days in the stocks at his home town.

The second charge was the kidnapping and attempted murder of Tom and me. This could have been for our *actual* murder, except for my totally fortuitous decision not to accompany Tom to the fight on Patrick Street! For this charge, the judge sentenced Dick Loone to three year's gaol.

On the final charge, that of arranging for nine dangerous criminals to escape from gaol, Loone was handed a sentence of two additional years; he is now in the lock-up at Campbell Town.

In the end, we had obtained the real names of most members of Robert's Force. They could have been considered guilty of treason too, but I went to their various territories and proposed to their Elders that they be held up to ridicule. Their names were made public and no members of the Force went on trial.

I also spoke of Wayne's situation during my travels around the Clans and I have the feeling that his case will be taken up sympathetically.

Tim the sheep farmer from Ross deserves praise for his friendship and for his very valuable support of Tom and me. Kinjo told me that he gave one of his Buddhism books to Tim.

All the families at Government House and Parliament House returned to their seasonal routines and Brutus went back to minding the farm animals and chasing possums whenever he has the chance.

Tom and I had a discussion last week. I suggested that Tom take over the crop area on my farm and that I help Tom on his farm and that we ask Kinjo to help the two of us in this endeavour. All up, we would jointly manage around 50 hectares. Kinjo headed off to talk this offer through with Lulo, who I'm told is a very nice girl. Tom suggested that we should invite John and Mary at Nowhere Else to come and join us. This could be a convenient way to pass our farms on to the younger generations.

Tom had the nerve to propose that we go to Paradise in May next year, *just to be sure*, but I made out that I did not hear him.

THE END

Further Reading

Aboriginal History:
a)www.janesoceania.com/australia_aboriginal_iceage_walktotasma-
nia/index1.htm Revised 24thMay, 2012
b) Yuval Harari, *Sapiens: A brief history of Humankind*, Harvill
Secker, London 2014
c) James Boyce, *Van Diemen's Land*, Black Inc., Melbourne 2008
Buddhism:
d) *The Teaching of Buddha*, publ. Bukkyo Dendo Kyokai, 1985,
ISBN: 9784892372148
Crusades:
e) W & A Durant, *The Story of Civilization – Vol. 4*, Simon and
Schuster, 1950
f) See https://en.wikipedia.org/wiki/Crusades, 6 June, 2018
Economic Systems in 20th & 21st Centuries:
g) Paul Mason, *Post Capitalism – A Guide to Our Future*, Allen
Lane, 2015
h) Olivier Berruyer, www.the-crises.com December 2010
Evolution of Education:
i) Alvin Gouldner, *The Future of Intellectuals and the rise of the New
Class*, Continuum Publishing Corporation, New York, 1979
j) Alston Chase, *In a Dark Wood*, Transaction Publications, New
York, 2001, pp3-5
k) HR Bowen et al, *Investment in Learning: The Individual and
Social Value of American Higher Education*, Jossey-Bass Inc., San
Francisco 1977
Farm Automation:
l) See Jim Lane, www.biofuelsdigest.com/bdigest/2015/08/09/the-
farm-of-the-future-utopia-or-dystopia-part-1-of-5/
Financial Crash of 2008:
m) Michael Lewis, *The Big Short*, Penguin Group (Australia), 2016
Greek Democracy:
n) See https://en.wikipedia.org/wiki/Athenian_democracy, 4 June

2018
Irish History:
o) Mary Cusack, *An Illustrated History of Ireland From AD400 to 1800*, First publ. 1868. Re-published by Bracken Books, London, 1995
Island History:
p) *Griffith REVIEW*, No. 39, Autumn 2013
q) James Boyce, *Van Diemen's Land*, Black Inc., Melbourne 2008
Legislative Council History:
r) WA Townsley, *The Struggle for Self-Government in Tasmania: 1842-1856*, Government Printer, Tasmania, 1951
s) *Royal Commission into the Tasmanian Constitution Act 1934*, Transcript of Proceedings – Volume 1, December 1981 + March 1982
Life Insurance Industry:
t) Adele Ferguson, *The Age*, 2 April 2016

Aboriginal names
(see http://tacinc.com.au/tasmanian-aboriginal-place-names/)
August 2019

Original Legislative Council District	New Clan Territory after boundary adjustments	Aboriginal name refers to:
Prosser	Trayapana	Spring Bay
Sorell	Premadena	Port Arthur
Derwent	Yingina	Great Lake